NIMBY UNIVERSE COLLECTION, VOLUME 1

TRAVELER'S TALES

LEAH R CUTTER

KNOTTED ROAD PRESS

NIMBY Universe Collection
Volume 1
Traveler's Tales

Published by Knotted Road Press
www.KnottedRoadPress.com

ID 4361280 © Amlyd | Dreamstime.com

ISBN: 978-1-64470-281-9

Come someplace new…
Are you a traveler? Do you enjoy exploring strange new worlds, new cultures, new people?

Journey into the various lands envisioned by Leah Cutter.

Sign up for my newsletter and I'll start you on your travels with a free copy of my book, *The Island Sampler*.

I will never spam you or use your email for nefarious purposes. You can also unsubscribe at any time.

http://www.LeahCutter.com/newsletter/

ALSO BY LEAH R CUTTER

Urban/Contemporary Fantasy Series

The Witch's Progress

Circle of Air

Circle of Fire

Circle of Water

Circle of Earth

Seattle Trolls

The Changeling Troll

The Princess Troll

The Fairy-Bridge Troll

The Troll-Demon War

The Troll-Human War

The Troll-Troll War

The Cassie Stories

Poisoned Pearls

Tainted Waters

Spoiled Harvest

Bloodied Ice

The Shadow Wars Trilogy

The Raven and the Dancing Tiger

The Guardian Hound

War Among the Crocodiles

The Clockwork Fairy Kingdom

The Clockwork Fairy Kingdom

The Maker, the Teacher, and the Monster

The Dwarven Wars

The Chronicles of Franklin

Franklin Versus The Popcorn Thief

Franklin Versus The Soul Thief

Franklin Versus The Child Thief

Epic Fantasy Series

Houses of the Dead

Houses Divided

Houses Fallen

Houses Reborn

Forgotten Gods

A Wind Blown Torment

A Stone Strewn Clash

A Sea Washed Victory

The Tanesh Empire Trilogy

The Glass Magician

The Desert Heart

The Ghost Dog

Huli Intergalactic: Science/Space Fantasy

Origins

The Strawberry Girl

Mysteries

The Purloined Letter Opener

Dancer in Darkness

Trophy Hunters

The Alvin Goodfellow Case Files

The Rabbit Mysteries

The Shredded Veil Mysteries

Mystery, Crime, and Mayhem

CONTENTS

INTRODUCTION

One of the problems that I have with fantasy that's set in a modern setting is this: If magic exists, why are there so many problems still with the real world? Why hasn't magic fixed everything that's wrong with our world?

The NIMBY stories are my attempt to begin to answer that. (And yes, NIMBY stands for Not In My Back Yard.) The fairies, brownies, and pixies, also known as the FBP, came out of hiding in the 1960s and 1970s, participating (instigating) the All Race riots in the US and other places.

In the present day, the FBP and humanity, at least in most parts of the US, have come to an understanding.

Humans have their world taken care of. There is no homelessness, as the FBP wouldn't stand for it. Same with polution. Those who tried to get around the rules found all that garbage dumped in their own backyards. Pipelines didn't get built across the wildness because the projects would be sabatogued by creatures the humans had no hope of fighting.

But everything is not idylic. In the suburbs, where

many of these stories take place, humans have made a bargain with the fae.

In return for their lawns being immaculant, their gardens lush, and the forests taken care of, the humans can only occupy those areas during the day. Including their backyards.

Once the sunsets, they are the property of the fae.

And woe be to the poor shmuck who sneaks out or who believes that he or she is beyond the rules.

There will continue to be NIMBY stories. I have far too much fun. And these stories, despite some of the darker undertones, are still very light.

At some point, I'll end up writing some of the darker aspects. Maybe for volume 2.

In the meanwhile, enjoy the silly, lighter side of fairy magic.

Leah R Cutter
Ravensdale, WA
May, 2022

THE FAIRY BOY-BAND

OSWALD SAT, ensconced in his favorite chair, next to the cheerily burning fireplace. He had a glass of his favorite scotch warming on the small end table beside him. The snifter was also a favorite: antique, hand-blown Tiffany glassware, with an indentation on one side that fit his thumb perfectly when he picked up the glass and swirled the amber liquor. His dad had given Oswald a full set of them for his thirtieth birthday, then died of a heart attack unexpectedly just a year later, which made Oswald cherish the glasses even more.

The scent of Oswald's simple dinner of poached salmon in white wine and dill lingered in the air, though overlaid now with the smell of woodsy, pine smoke. Oswald still wore his office clothes—plain blue long-sleeved shirt and tan-colored slacks—but he'd taken his shoes off and donned his heaviest wool socks to ward off the chill of the autumn evening.

Everything was perfect. Silence surrounded him, so welcome after the hectic day in the office where he worked as a quality engineer, testing the code of morons. He had a new book to read—a fascinating non-fiction work about the history of pixie engineering. He was settled in for the night, no lights on in his living room except for the fire (loving his electronic book reader!), and at peace. No girlfriend badgering him, no new video games demanding to be played, no awkward social situation that he needed to engage in for his work.

Nope. Just him, a book, a good scotch, and the quiet of the evening.

Until the damned music started to play.

Oswald tried to ignore the tinkling, which to his ears sounded like the musician tapped on a series of icicles, going from tiny to large, testing their tone but all of them annoyingly tinny. Then came the sweeping flute, the trilling noises worse than claws down a chalkboard, making him shiver.

Of course, tonight the band had added some sort of bass that sounded like frogs belching and farting.

With a huge, put upon sigh, Oswald set his reader on the end table and picked up his scotch again. He couldn't go complain to the fairies making music in his backyard that he had a headache again. They didn't have to accommodate him every time he made that excuse, and he'd much rather save it for when he *was* actually ill.

The arrangement with the fairies had all been written out in clear language in the agreement that he'd signed when he'd bought his house. He owned the building and the land it sat on, though he had to check with the neighborhood home owner's association (HOA) first before he painted his house or added large decorations. He could use his house and the land as he saw fit during the day and early evening. If he gave adequate notice, he could also use the yard later at night, say, for a celebration or ritual.

However, the fairies owned the backyard starting one hour after true night had fallen, which meant during the fall and winter, like now, they'd start playing their damned music earlier and earlier.

He'd complained to the association about the racket the fairies made every night. The association came by and merely ensured that the fairies were in compliance with "quiet hours." Now, the stupid band started their jam session strictly on time, one hour after full dark, as well as ended exactly at 11:00 P.M.

Oswald had no ideas that fairies could be so punctual —they tended to work on their own, "fairy" time. He did know they could be assholes. He'd worked with one for a while, a stupid prima donna developer who'd believed his code was perfect and never needed to be tested.

Thankfully, the idiot had left to form his own company. (Oswald would never admit to how small his soul was and how gleefully he'd watched the asshole's company sink.)

Fairies had always lived beside humanity, along with brownies and pixies. (Elves, trolls, vampires, and all the other creatures man had documented over the years had turned out to be just myths, thankfully, even though the consensus about ghosts was far from unanimous.) However, it hadn't been until the civil rights movement in the 1960s that the FBP (fairies, brownies, pixies) came forward and demanded equal rights as well.

The denial had been truly epic, particularly on the part of the US Government. The backlash had been immediate as well. However, after the All Races riots in the 1970s, an accord was signed and everyone went back to making gobs of money in the 1980s—including the fairies and other races.

However, while the FBP could all cast glamours and appear to be human-sized, in reality, they didn't grow much taller than up to a man's knee. They had no use for houses, cars, or TV, living on the magical plane. They did like the internet, and Oswald had once seen a commercial for a documentary about FBP online addiction.

So the FBP frequently worked out deals like the one Oswald had signed, time-sharing yards, parks, or wilderness areas. They also paid rent, keeping the area tidy and beautiful, which made the properties cheaper. It also meant that no one littered anymore: fairies would likely take any trash a human dumped in one of their areas and make it magically appear inside the human's house at the most inopportune moment.

While there had been talk of forming an environmental protection agency, once the FBP came forward, there was no need. They wouldn't allow land to be despoiled anymore. Any grand engineering scheme the humans came up with, like oil pipelines or drilling offshore, had to be okayed by the FBP. Of course, greedy corporations tried to get around that, only to have their operations plagued with inexplicable accidents, so many that they'd end up scrapping the project.

The air Oswald breathed was crystal clean and fresh. The sidewalks he walked down were empty of trash. He'd heard that in areas where the FBP weren't as well liked or as well integrated, people without homes actually lived on the streets. He couldn't imagine that. The FBP had been good for humanity, in general.

However, he hated the racket the fairies who lived in his backyard made. Every. Single. Night. It was driving him batty. They played the same songs over and over again, practicing.

What could he do to evict them?

THE NEXT MORNING, while waiting for his garlic bagels to finish toasting, Oswald checked online for FBP neighborhood "support" groups. What he found turned his stomach. He wasn't a racist, or a species-ist, not like those crazy people. And he wasn't about to move to Alabama or some such "humans only" state, though how in the hell people were able to ensure that, he had no idea.

There was an old joke about fairies breeding like bunnies. The truth was that there was no place in the world immune from their influence.

Oswald's own HOA had been useless regarding getting the noise turned down. He spread cream cheese on his bagel, then set it aside and let it melt while he poured himself a cup of coffee from the automated pot on his kitchen counter.

He knew he couldn't get rid of the fairies, as much as he might like to. He'd thought about buying huge, six foot tall speakers and using them to blast music into the backyard and drown out the fairy music.

However, that didn't actually get rid of his problem. He wanted less noise, not more. He'd looked into noise cancelation headphones, but none of those would guarantee blocking the music of the fey, which operated on more than just human dimensions.

Oswald continued doing random searches on the internet while he stood at the kitchen counter eating his breakfast. He looked at fairy bands (who knew that fairy boy-bands were so popular?), equipment for dealing with fairy noise (all of it designed to part a fool from his money) as well as old myths for dealing with fairies, like leaving out a thimbleful of milk and cookie crumbs (though fairies appeared to prefer cake crumbs to cookies).

As Oswald rinsed off his dishes, he thought about the last time he'd gone out to try to get the fairies to shut up. Fairies lived to be about a hundred years old, and unless they were using a glamour, tended to look their age. In addition, the younger fairies glowed with a particularly clean white light. From all the inter-species classes Oswald had been required to attend from grade school onward, he knew that older fairies had a more yellowish glow to them.

The lead singer Oswald had talked with had been young, with a searing white glow. Oswald would have put him in his early twenties. He had a very pale face with a sharp nose and chin. He'd dyed his hair green and worn a torn T-shirt in a futile attempt to look tough. His wings had been amazing, though, iridescent blue and gold, more like a dragonfly's wings than an angel's. (Fairies always appeared with their wings no matter what size or shape they took. No one really understood if it was racial pride or trait even glamours couldn't disguise.)

The lead singer had also been incredibly argumentative, not wanting to hear any of Oswald's complaints, claiming that they'd been their first and that they'd only permitted Oswald to live there.

The fairy had been very careful not to make any threats. Fairies were good with language that way.

Maybe Oswald could talk to the head of the fairies in the neighborhood. He wasn't getting anywhere with the kids. His HOA had a fairy liaison he could schedule a meeting with. Oswald had merely talked with the human representative before.

Perhaps, if Oswald could speak with another adult, he could finally get some peace and quiet.

He scheduled an appointment online, for later that evening, at Margaret's Coffee Shop, just down the street.

It made him feel better as he waited for the company bus to take him to his job. He was finally taking positive steps instead of hiding in his house, shaking with rage.

Then again, if this didn't work, maybe he would try one of those illegal sonic disrupters that would force the fairies to leave.

OSWALD HURRIED from the bus stop directly to the coffee shop. He'd planned on arriving early, but traffic had thwarted him. Luckily, he was close to being on time, within a few minutes.

The shop door banged open as Oswald rushed in. The barista standing behind the counter that ran along the right wall glared at him, though no one else appeared to notice. To his left, over a dozen tables spread out across the bare concrete floor, most of them occupied with either FBP or humans, chatting and laughing. Two balls of rainbow-colored light, each about the size of a volleyball, flitted above a pair of older fairies sitting at the back—very young, small fairies, playing. Beside them stood a tiny, empty stage, with posters advertising local bands playing on the weekends as well as an upcoming poetry slam.

A glowering, older fairy sat by himself at a table very close to the entrance. Oswald rushed over and asked expectantly, "Are you Francesco?"

The fairy looked up. He had a pushed in face, like a pug, with black eyes and hair. He looked Hispanic, with dark skin and broad features. Even his hands appeared meaty where they lay on the table. His wings, too, appeared yellowed and aged. He wore a dark blue T-shirt that showed more chest muscles than the usual fairy, and clean blue jeans, with black work boots.

Was this how he really looked? Or was it some elaborate glamour to make him seem like a working class dude?

"Frank," the fairy said in a voice that was much deeper than Oswald expected.

"Can I get you anything?" Oswald asked, gesturing toward the empty counter where the barista still glared at him, expectant.

"Two crumb cakes," Frank said after a moment.

"Sure thing. Coming right up," Oswald said, trying to hide his excitement. Was this a way to bribe the fairy? Maybe get him to see reason?

Oswald ordered himself a hot mocha and two cakes for Frank, then stayed at the counter, watching the barista carefully. She seemed like the type to spit in a drink if she decided she didn't like you. And right now, Oswald would swear that she not only hated all of humanity but every single creature on the planet. The hair curling around her face radiated rage. Her dark skin looked flushed, and her broad features appeared chiseled in angry stone.

But she made his drink competently enough, even added extra whipped cream without charging him for it. It was far beyond her to smile or act polite. However, she did wear a nametag that labeled her as "Margret" and the coffee shop was named "Margret's Coffee Shop." Was she the owner?

Oswald hurried back with his goodies to the table where Frank sat. Margaret had served the cakes on a small pewter plate that easily fit into Oswald's palm. The cakes, too, were tiny, about as big as the end of Oswald's thumb. They were made with almond meal, lavender, and honey.

After Oswald took off his coat, he realized that Frank was waiting for him to say something.

"Thank you for meeting me, tonight," Oswald said hurriedly.

"I don't have a lot of time," Frank replied. He broke the tiny golden cake in front of him into pieces, scattering the crumbs. Then he pressed his thumb onto the plate, picking up the crumbs and licking them off.

Oswald tried not to be grossed out by the fairy's eating habits. He reminded himself that no matter how large this Frank may appear, he was actually tiny, and more than mere crumbs wouldn't fit into his mouth.

"Then I'll get right to the point," Oswald said. "I have this fairy band who plays music in my backyard every night."

Frank pierced him with a sharp look. "They playing outside of regular haunting hours?" he asked.

"No, but they make such a racket! Every single night," Oswald said. "Surely we could work out a deal where they only played a few nights a week." He would prefer for them to go play somewhere else, *anywhere* else, but he knew he couldn't just insist that they vacate.

"What would you offer?" Frank asked. He didn't sound sympathetic, but at least he'd asked, instead of saying it was impossible, like the HOA rep had.

"I don't know," Oswald said. He hadn't considered what the fairies might want from him. "I could supply crumb cakes or something." How much was his peace and quiet worth? How much would the fairies try to bleed him dry?

"Case of dew-drop wine, delivered every fortnight," Frank said after a moment.

Oswald gulped. He couldn't afford that! A single bottle cost about what he made in a day, and he made a very good wage working in IT.

"A bottle, once a month," Oswald countered. He'd never been good at bargaining, though he knew he must.

Frank snorted. "Don't waste my time. A full case. Every fourteen days."

"What exactly would I get if I could meet your price?" Oswald asked. He knew he'd have to spell everything out exactly. Fairies were notoriously tricky that way.

A look of cunning crossed Frank's face. "Music every other night," he said.

"No," Oswald said. "That's still too much. Music once a week, for two bottles a month."

Frank shook his head. "Not worth it," he said.

"What do you mean?" Oswald asked as Frank licked more crumbs away. God, he wasn't about to lick the plate clean, was he?

Frank pierced him with a look. "You know that if they aren't practicing in your yard, they'll set up a garage in the fairy lands and play?" He shuddered. "The agreement lets them play here, so they aren't driving their parents batty with the noise. If you want them to play elsewhere, you've got to make it worth our while."

Oswald gulped. Crap. He couldn't afford the bribe Frank wanted, not without going into debt. While fairies normally would negotiate, he knew Frank wouldn't budge.

"Can't you just make them stop?" Oswald asked.

Frank rolled his eyes at him. "Have you ever tried to get a teenager to do what you wanted?"

Oswald opened his mouth then closed it again. He didn't have kids, had never wanted them. On the other hand, coders frequently behaved like a bunch of juvenile delinquents. He felt Frank's pain.

"Then how am I going to get some peace and quiet?" Oswald asked.

Frank shrugged and stood up. "Your problem, human. Not ours." The fairy suddenly shrank back down as he lifted off the ground, hovering directly in front of Oswald's face. "The agreement you signed states that as long as the kids stick to the quiet hours, they get to play. Nothing you can do about it. You can't make us."

With that, Frank flitted off, passing through the glass door of the shop like a shot.

Oswald felt himself grinding his teeth. Damn it! What was he going to do?

"I hate it when they do that."

Oswald turned around to look up at Margaret. She still glared at the closed door. "Did you see the way the glass shakes? I'm always afraid that they're going to shatter it. God, I hate the FBP some days."

Oswald nodded in sympathy. "Was there something in particular they did to you today?" he asked. He normally wouldn't have engaged her, or anyone. But he felt like grousing with another human about the injustice of it all, as well as the awfulness of all fairies.

Margaret nodded. "The fairy band I had scheduled to have play here for the next couple months just broke up. They can't get their shit together long enough to send even one of the fairies to play an acoustic set or anything." She grimaced. "I had a bunch of publicity lined up and everything."

Oswald blinked, surprised. Why in the hell would she want any sort of fairy music in her café? The question must have showed on his face.

"Fairy music gets on my nerves too, but they sure draw a crowd. And they're cheap to feed. I make a good profit," Margaret said.

Oswald nodded, a plan forming, his day suddenly brightening. "I might be able to help..."

OSWALD STOOD at the back of the packed coffee shop as the band, *Nimby*, took the stage. The "xylophone" that one member of the band played was, in fact, made out of what looked like icicles, glistening blue and white spikes that hung in the air in front of her. The lead singer strutted around on the tiny stage like a testosterone-driven frat boy, playing his flute suggestively and making at least the girl fairies swoon. Oswald had no idea what to call the instrument the bass player had. It looked like a combination bagpipe and sitar, that he strummed, squeezed, and blew on all at the same time.

Margaret gave him the thumbs up from behind the counter, though she was too busy to talk with him. She'd even had to hire extra help for the evenings the band played.

As part of their agreement, Oswald always took in the first five minutes of "music" before returning to his peace and quiet. He wasn't sure why the fairies had insisted on that in their negotiations.

But seeing how he and Margaret were getting along and chatting almost every day, perhaps it wasn't the worst condition.

He'd been more than happy to agree to find them other gigs, once this one ended, as long as they stayed out of backyard most nights. They'd even given him a cut of their take, just one percent, to make it worth his time.

Plus, the band seemed to treat him differently, now. They ran their playlists by him, letting him change the order of the songs so they didn't get monotonous, taking his suggestions of mixing fast songs with slow ones so they'd appeal to a wider audience.

The music itself still set his teeth on edge. It was worse than two cats in heat fighting, yowling, squeaking, and hissing. He'd never get used to it—hipsters who claimed they were "into" FBP bands were lying. The music of the fey was unsettling to humans: that was just their nature.

Oswald stayed for two whole songs before disappearing back into the late fall night. Leaves swirled around his feet, dancing to the tune of the winds. The crisp air filled his lungs and nipped at his nose and cheeks. He was so looking forward to a peaceful evening at home!

He hurried on his way, already tasting the smoky scotch he planned on pouring.

Except that a young fairy boy awaited him, standing on his doorstep and looking forlorn.

"Can I help you?" Oswald said as he walked up the short sidewalk to his door.

The boy looked up. He had golden, spiky hair, dark skin, and blue-green eyes that shone with sadness. "Can you help me too?" he asked. Only then did he pull down the guitar he'd had slung across his back. "I'm a singer/songwriter," he explained, strumming a chord.

Oswald couldn't help his shiver. Though it was a human instrument, the sound still carried echoes of dark dances in fairyland.

"I'm looking for a place to gig," the boy explained after another few chords. "Can you help me?"

"Pop music?" Oswald asked after the boy played a few bouncy chords.

He sniffed, insulted. "Indie. Can you help? Find me a place to play?"

Oswald blinked. His future suddenly unfurled before him.

Music manager for the fey. He'd still be working for prima donnas, but he was used to that.

"I'll meet you in the backyard," Oswald said after a moment. He knew better than to invite any fairy across the threshold of his house. "Maybe we can arrange something."

After the boy turned and started trundling around the house, Oswald hurried inside, poured himself a snifter full of scotch, then poured out a few drops of milk into a handy thimble.

Margaret surely knew other coffee shop owners who wanted exotic music. There were always hipster weddings, too. And dance parties.

The possibilities were endless.

Even if it meant he'd be dealing with fairies and having to listen to their damned music for the rest of his life.

THE ICE SKATING FAIRY

"GEEZ, THIS BITES."

Cindy looked around. Who had just voiced the exact words going through her head? She hadn't heard anyone come up behind her. She looked down both sides the row of seats where she sat, as well as behind her. The empty seats of the arena stretched out in both directions until they curved away.

Cindy repositioned her earmuffs, careful not to get stray pieces of her brown hair caught in them and end up looking like a dork. She'd worn the neon-blue earmuffs today, the ones that matched the warm gloves she wore. Her bright-green down jacket kept out most of the cold, though Cindy was used to the frigid temperatures of the practice rink. More than once Cindy's coach had told Cindy that the chilled air gave her pale cheeks a nice, healthy, pink glow, as a way of derailing her grousing. Plus, the color hid her totally typical teenage acne. Black ski pants covered her legs, the kind that zipped at the bottom so she could wear them over her cast.

On the ice of the skating rink in front of her, Janice was *still* not picking up the choreography. It wasn't that difficult. Turn, turn, leap, camel. Cindy could do this simple of a routine in her sleep. She couldn't help but roll her eyes as Janice stumbled again. Cindy sighed. Wouldn't Janice *ever* figure this out?

Then Cindy turned to glare at the crutches resting against the seat beside her.

Could have done this sort of routine. Before her stupid sister and her stupid friends had agreed to drive Cindy to practice, only to slam into the back of a stopped pickup truck. At least no one had ended up permanently damaged. Cindy, though, had gotten the worst of the injuries: a fractured tibia.

Which meant she couldn't practice. Couldn't *perform.*

Wasn't going to be going be part of the annual mid-winter jubilee celebration put on by the best teen figure skaters in the state of Washington.

Was stuck on the sidelines, kissing nationals goodbye. As well as any chance of qualifying for the Olympics this year…

Just beyond Cindy's metal crutches she saw something glowing with a clean, white light, as though a rogue spotlight had directed its beam there.

It took Cindy a moment to realize it wasn't something shining that way, but rather, some*one*.

A fairy.

The fairy looked like a regular fairy, with a sharp nose, thin lips, high cheekbones, and a pointed chin. Cindy instantly envied the fairy's clear, acne-free skin, the color somewhere between gold and bronze. The fairy's black hair had French braids along the sides of her head, then was all gathered together into an impressively thick braid that went halfway down her back, a dark black line between her yellow-and-white gossamer wings.

Cindy had missed the fairy the first time she'd looked around because the fairy barely came up past the handles of Cindy's crutches. Like all fairies, this one was diminutive, maybe eighteen inches tall when she stood. Of course, fairies could use magic to seem as big as a human, though she'd always have her wings, no matter what her appearance.

The fairy wasn't wearing a jacket, despite how cold the arena was kept. Instead, she had on a tight, white, sleeveless top that showed how bony her chest was, and a short, white-and-blue satin skirt. Blue-and-white striped stockings covered her legs, and she wore bright-blue ice skates that were so tiny they looked like blueberries.

The fairy gave a rather loud sigh and waved toward

Janice, who'd fallen down (again!) and was slowing getting back up. "Just look at that."

"I know. Pitiful. Right?" Cindy said, working to maintain the appropriate level of teenager disgust in her voice and not excitement. She'd never talked with a fairy before, not personally like this. She'd seen them at school during the inter-species classes she'd been required to attend, and occasionally at Commodore Park when she'd been hanging out with her friends, but that was it.

Her family lived in an old rambler, built back in the early 70s, before the fairies, brownies, and pixies (FBP) started signing time-sharing agreements with humans. Mankind would get to use their outdoor spaces during daylight hours, while the FBP took them over at night, in exchange for keeping them pristine and lush.

No one Cindy knew had any fairy friends, not like those TV shows, such as "Frankie and the Fairy". Cindy's family lived north of Seattle where fairies weren't as common. Plus, it wasn't as if any of the FBP attended the same schools or went out to the same restaurants as humans. Though Cindy had heard about this one coffee shop that now had a fairy boy-band playing regularly…

"I could have done a much better job," the fairy grumbled, waving her hand toward Janice and the rink.

"You?" Cindy asked, astonished. "You skate?"

The fairy rolled her eyes at Cindy. "No, I just like the cosplay of dressing up like a figure skater. Of course, I skate."

Cindy blinked, still surprised. "I didn't know fairies skated. Do you compete?"

The fairy sighed and shook her head. "Not enough interest in the community to get a competitive circuit going."

"I'm sorry," Cindy said. If she couldn't compete…she

didn't know what she would have done. Perfecting her routine and performing for the judges was as much a part of her life as breathing.

"I came here today to audition for your position," the fairy said. "But the officials claimed I would have an unfair advantage. You know. With the magic and flying and all."

"But couldn't you agree to not use your magic or your wings while performing?" Cindy asked. She felt flattered that the fairy had wanted to be in the mid-winter jubilee.

"That's what I said!" the fairy said, slapping her hand against the hard plastic of the seat, making a tiny sound despite how much emphasis she used. "But the officials didn't have a way to test for my magical ability, so they said no."

"Wouldn't your people have a way to verify that you'd kept your promise?" Cindy asked cautiously, fascinated by this glimpse into actual real fairies and not the crap they showed on TV.

"The officials didn't trust them either," the fairy groused. "They needed an 'impartial' panel."

"That's so unfair," Cindy said.

"I know, right?" the fairy said. "I'm Belinda, by the way."

"Cindy," she replied. She knew better than to stick her hand out or something. Fairies didn't shake hands, not like humans. Something about magic making it uncomfortable to touch mundanes.

"I'd love to see you skate, sometime," Cindy added shyly after a moment.

Belinda gave her a sharp grin. "I did convince the assholes that they had to give me practice time. Regular, human practice ends at 10 PM, and I can have the rink after that. Want to come watch?"

Cindy bit her lips together. Normally, that was way

past her bedtime. However, she wasn't competing right now. She could cheat a little on her sleep. "I'd love to."

"Great. See you tonight," Belinda said. Then she flew off, a bright white streak running high along the rows of the arena.

For a moment, Cindy thought that Belinda might turn and fly over the ice, maybe do a strafing run over Janice, see if she could get the girl to fall again. However, Belinda merely disappeared at the far wall, where the arena curved.

Janice fell soon after anyway.

CINDY WAITED by the end of the arena, her injured leg raised on the seat in front of her, her crutches to the side. Though sometimes practice did go until 10 PM, no one was actually out on the ice. She'd gotten to the rink a little early, but was disappointed when she didn't find anyone there.

Still, she was determined to wait. She shivered a little, despite being dressed for the cold with her black ski pants, bright red down jacket that night, and brilliant white gloves and earmuff covered in long fake fur.

Exactly at 10 PM, Belinda appeared.

Cindy couldn't help but jump. One moment, she was by herself, watching videos on her phone, the next, Belinda was hovering directly beside her.

"Good! You're here!" Belinda said. She sounded relieved.

Had Belinda thought that Cindy wouldn't show up?

"Of course," Cindy said. "I really wanted to see you skate." No one she knew had ever seen a fairy skate.

Belinda beamed at Cindy. She wore the same outfit she'd had on earlier, though now, it, too, seemed to have its own glow, the white sleeveless top covered in glittering rhinestones, the blue-and-white satin skirt lined in bright light, the tiny blue skates pulsing with neon. "Come out onto the ice with me," Belinda said. "Let me give you the best seat in the house."

Cindy bit her lips together, then nodded. She felt like a dork on the ice with crutches. But she'd figured out how to do it, moving very slowly so she wouldn't fall. She had a full walking cast and wouldn't graduate to a shorter one for a couple weeks.

And while Belinda didn't seem like the being with the most patience in the world, Cindy was still going to go slow. She stood up, grabbed her crutches, and made her way to the entrance, doing her best to ignore the impatient ball of light vibrating over her left shoulder.

The world opened up for Cindy as soon as she stepped onto the ice. *This* was her home. She felt alive on the white face of the rink, while everything else, all her troubles and cares, just faded away.

She wished with all her heart that she could glide away from this spot, taking sweeping steps and skate all around the rink. Instead, she planted her crutches, swung forward carefully, paused, balanced, then brought her crutches around.

Belinda hovered in the air beside Cindy, at head height. "I knew you were injured," the fairy said, her voice holding many questions.

Cindy nodded. "Car accident. Broken tibia. It'll heal and I'll compete again next year." She was keeping herself in shape with primarily upper body work. Coach had told her that stronger arms would help her with her lifts.

"Must suck losing a year," Belinda said.

"It does," Cindy admitted. Then she shrugged. "Can't

do much about that, though. Unless the FBP have healing powers they've never shared?"

Belinda looked startled for a moment, as if she hadn't expected to be teased. Then she gave a snorting laugh. "As if." She grew serious. "My magic is mainly for illusions and glamours. Not much else."

"I still think it's cool," Cindy said.

Belinda rolled her eyes. "Yeah, whatever." She paused for a moment, before flying closer to Cindy. "Don't tell anyone, ever, but I think it's kind of cool as well."

Cindy nodded, understanding. Some days, controlling her enthusiasm was the only thing that made her feel like an adult.

When they were about one quarter of the way across the rink, Belinda stopped and asked, "Should I skate in this form? Or be bigger?"

Cindy thought for a moment. "I'd like to see both," she said. "First, human sized, then your natural size."

Belinda nodded.

Cindy jumped for a second time that night when suddenly, a full-sized figure skater stood beside her. The illusion body looked exactly like Belinda, with the white top fitting her well (and still showing more bones than muscles), the skirt hanging in lovely blue and white stripes, the muscles in her long legs outlined by the stripes in her tights, and her brilliantly blue ice skates shining with their own light.

Belinda did a slow turn, letting Cindy see all sides of her. Belinda's wings had grown as well. They seemed more like large dragonfly wings than butterfly wings. Cindy knew that different fairies had different types, and while there was speculation about what the different types signified, no one knew for certain and the fairies weren't telling. Belinda's wings sparkled with gold, as if sprinkled with radioactive glitter.

"You look gorgeous," Cindy said truthfully.

"Good enough for competition?" Belinda asked.

Cindy heard the catch in Belinda's voice, though the fairy was trying to play it cool. "I think so," Cindy said. She examined the fairy's skirt critically. "The satin isn't too heavy to lift when you twirl, is it?"

Belinda responded by suddenly spinning in place. The skirt lifted beautifully, just like it was supposed to.

However, no skater could just turn that way. They needed momentum to achieve a spin. The only way Belinda had managed it was by using magic.

"What?" Belinda asked when she stopped and faced Cindy again.

"The spin was great," Cindy said, feeling awkward.

"But, what?" Belinda asked. "Your face is all funny. Like you're trying to hold in a fart."

That made Cindy giggle. "Okay. I'll tell you. But you can't get mad at me for telling you the truth." That was one thing that her inter-species classes had all emphasized: while fairies might look mostly human, they weren't. Fairies could be spiteful, and many had a volatile temper.

"You used magic to go into that spin, right?" Cindy asked. She hurried on. "It's okay, it's cool, it's just us. But that spin was fueled by magic."

Belinda blinked at Cindy. "Yeah, I suppose. I didn't even think about it. That's just part of how I skate."

Was this what the officials had seen? That magic was so natural to Belinda that she couldn't skate without it?

"Do you want to show me the routine you did for the officials?" Cindy asked. "Or do you have a different performance piece?"

Belinda nodded, still deep in thought. "I have a couple pieces," she said slowly. "Do you want to see them?"

"Sure!" Cindy said. That was why she'd come here tonight, to watch a fairy skate.

Belinda stood where she was for a moment longer. "These pieces…I'm still using magic in them."

"That's cool," Cindy said. And it was. Her friends were going to be sooooo jealous that Cindy got to see a fairy not only skate, but do magic while performing.

"It just never occurred to me that I shouldn't use magic while I'm skating," Belinda said, her words rushed together.

Cindy nodded. She wasn't sure what was wrong, but before she could ask, the first few notes of "The Dance of the Sugar Plum Fairies" came tinkling over the PA system and Belinda took off.

It took Cindy all she had to not giggle at Belinda's musical choice.

Then the music changed subtly. Over the top of the lighter notes came an even higher melody. Cindy shivered. The music of the fae intermingled with the familiar human song. The effect was unsettling, as if it was the same tune being played on instruments slightly off key.

Cindy had heard before that fairy music couldn't be appreciated by humans. She'd scoffed at that, figuring that sort of opinion came only from people like her parents, you know, *old* people. Younger people, like herself, could learn to enjoy it.

Now, she wondered if maybe they were right, if the music of the FBP was just too unnerving.

Belinda had slowly skated away, doing a buildup for her first leap. Of course, she reached heights no human could match, shooting up ten feet into the air and landing gently. She immediately went into an arabesque, followed by an amazingly quick camel spin.

Cindy found herself getting dizzy watching Belinda. There were no long, slow buildups. It was all leap, jump, spin.

In addition, while it was technically accurate, it was just a series of tricks that weren't connected together. And more importantly, Belinda didn't have a good sense of musicality. None of her leaps were timed to the song.

Abruptly, the piece ended. Belinda appeared in front of Cindy, who tried not to be too startled, afraid she'd end up on her ass on the ice.

"What did you think?" Belinda asked.

Cindy noted with a touch of jealousy that Belinda wasn't even out of breath.

"It was technically impressive," Cindy said cautiously. And it had been.

"I can hear that big old 'but' hanging out just there," Belinda said. She sounded angry.

It took Cindy a moment to find the right words. "It *was* technically impressive. All those leaps and spins. But it wasn't an emotional performance. You just—did tricks."

Belinda blinked, looking surprised. "Isn't that what I'm supposed to do?" she asked.

Cindy smiled. She remembered one of her first coaches not letting her skate to the music he'd chosen, but instead, making Cindy dance on the ice to the tune. She'd felt so awkward and out of control. She much preferred skating, gliding across the rink.

About halfway through the song, though, something had changed. Cindy found herself moving *to* the music, feeling it with her arms in a way she hadn't been when she'd merely been performing the choreography. She'd stopped caring how she looked and instead, let the music move her.

Every time she had new music, she spent time just dancing and moving to it, to get a feel for the tune and perform beyond the choreography.

"You must *feel* the music," Cindy told Belinda. "You're telling a story with your dance. The judges want to see you dance your heart out, and leave it all on the ice."

Belinda shook her head. "I've heard people say that before. I don't understand what it means."

"Do you like the song you used for your performance?" Cindy asked. It was appropriate, but not the easiest piece to skate to.

Belinda shrugged. "It's got a good rhythm."

Cindy blinked, puzzled. It didn't have a good beat, at least as far as she was concerned. "But what does that song represent to you? How does it make you feel?"

Belinda tilted her head to one side. "Humans are all about the emotional side of things, aren't they?"

Cindy nodded.

"Fairies—our emotions run just as deep. But they're here, and gone. Like a rainbow," Belinda said. "It would be difficult to connect to a song, and not just perform."

"But that's what performance is," Cindy argued. "Not just the notes for a singer. Or the steps for a dancer. It's what you, the artist, can bring to a piece."

"I've never considered it that way," Belinda admitted.

Cindy nodded while Belinda thought for a few moments.

"Can you help me?" Belinda asked, her words all rushed together. "Not just figure out a performance without magic. But how to be a better figure skater? And maybe get a second chance with the officials, and still perform in the mid-winter jubilee?"

"I'd love to," Cindy said. She'd always known that would be her path: from artist and performer (and hopefully, gold medal winner) to professional coach. Working with Belinda would be good practice for her.

"Do you want to start tonight?" Belinda asked. Now she sounded breathless, as if she'd been performing hard.

Cindy thought for a moment, then shook her head. "What I want you to do is to find some music that *means* something to you. Music that breaks your heart, or makes you want to dance with joy. Something that moves you."

"I know just the thing," Belinda said. "It's fairy music," she warned.

"It doesn't matter if I like it or not," Cindy said firmly. "You need to feel it. Then I can help you express yourself more."

Belinda rocked her head from side to side, considering. "I'll figure out a few pieces. See if there's something less disturbing for humans."

"Good," Cindy said. "Then, meet here again tomorrow night?"

Belinda gave her a huge grin. "Thought you'd never ask," she teased. The fairy shrank back down to her regular, diminutive size. "Thank you," she said seriously. Then she took off like a glittery rocket.

Cindy shook her head. She knew that ice didn't really have a scent. Still, it smelled like sweet victory to her.

Then she slowly, carefully, turned and started making her way across the ice. Her mom would be thrilled that Cindy had found a student. She'd been urging her daughter to start training other skaters. It would be a way of keeping her own skills up.

But Cindy also knew that her mom, her stupid older sister, and all of their collective friends had *never* imagined that Cindy would find someone like Belinda.

CINDY FROWNED as Belinda did another flying sit-spin. She got good verticality. One leg was straight out in front of her and the other was bent correctly, as if she was sitting on a chair. However, she maintained the position for a good two and a half rotations.

Far too long for a skater without magic.

After yet another quadruple axel, Cindy held up her arm, the signal she and Belinda had worked out to get Belinda to stop her progression. At least Cindy no longer had to use her crutches. She'd finally graduated to the short walking cast and it was easier for her to balance.

Belinda skated slowly over to where Cindy stood at the mid-line, the fairy's shoulders drooping and her head down. She knew why Cindy had stopped her.

Cindy wasn't sure how much more she could help the fairy. Belinda was starting to finally feel the music she moved to. It had turned out to be a good thing that the fairy tunes were so disturbing: it made Cindy focus on the dance, because as a human, she couldn't feel anything but uneasy. It also meant Belinda had to work twice as hard to express emotion in her routine.

They'd quickly discovered that Belinda was most convincing when it came to sad songs rather than happy or playful pieces.

However, Belinda couldn't seem to let go of her magic. She always forgot herself, particularly once she started showing more feelings in her performance.

"Magic again, huh?" Belinda asked as she drew closer.

Cindy nodded. "I'm sorry," she said. "I wonder if it's just too much a part of you."

Belinda sighed. "That's what Mom said. That trying to

give up my magic was like trying to cut off my wings. Can't do it, not and survive."

"I see," Cindy said. "I'm sorry," she said again. "I'm not sure what I can do to help."

"No, no!" Belinda said. "You've already helped me so much. I am a *much* better performer now. You can't be throwing in the towel on me."

"I'd love to keep working with you," Cindy said. "However, I'm not sure that we're ever going to have something to show the officials of the mid-winter jubilee." They'd scheduled another interview in just a few days.

"But I have to be able to perform there!" Belinda said.

"Why?" Cindy asked. She'd never understood why Belinda wanted to perform in a human spectacle. Though Cindy had asked before, she hadn't believed the story Belinda had made up about improving fairy-human relations.

Besides, didn't the fairies have their own great balls and parities at mid-winter? Wasn't it a special holiday for them? Why did Belinda want to miss it?

Belinda pressed her lips together as if debating whether or not to tell her coach. "My dad died earlier this year," the fairy said after a short while.

"That's horrible!" Cindy said. "I'm so sorry." She had no idea.

Belinda shrugged. "It's not like he was murdered or anything. It was a freak accident. The kind that aren't supposed to happen. He got caught in a plane engine turbine while he was flying. Tore his wings right off. Mom says he died instantly."

"Jeez," Cindy said. "I really am sorry."

Belinda nodded. "I *so* don't want to go to the mid-winter ball this year. Everyone will be staring at me, whispering about me and the *tragedy* of my life." She rolled her eyes so hard Cindy was surprised she didn't pull something. "It's sad, yes, that my dad is gone. I really loved him. But *he's* the one who died. Not me."

"Is that why you started figure skating?" Cindy asked. She knew that Belinda hadn't been performing for very long. She'd just watched videos of others skating. She'd never had a coach before. YouTube had been her teacher.

"Naw, I started last year. But Dad always encouraged me. Called me his icy glitter ball."

Cindy wasn't sure what that meant, but the endearment had appeared to be quite heartfelt, given the glint of tears in Belinda's eyes.

"I know you can't take my place in the jubilee," Cindy said slowly. Janice was finally starting to pick up the choreography. "But maybe you can perform on your own. Get a place as a special guest appearance, or something."

Belinda shook her head. "I'm a nobody. There isn't any draw to my name, you know? And none of the fairies would come to see me anyway. The jubilee is at the same time as the primary fairy ball."

"Then we'll have to come up with such an amazing performance that the officials will beg for you to be part of the jubilee anyway," Cindy said firmly.

Belinda nodded slowly. "Okay," she said. Her eyes had that far off look that she got when she was really concentrating. "I may have an idea. Meet me here tomorrow night."

"Same time, same channel?" Cindy asked, teasing. It had become a routine with them.

"You got it," Belinda said. "And bring your practice skates!" the fairy added just before she popped out of sight.

Her skates? Why would the fairy request that? Cindy hadn't touched her skates in weeks.

Sadness filled her. She *missed* skating so much. While

the coaching was great, particularly with such an athletic (and magical) student, it wasn't the same.

Still, Cindy would do as Belinda had asked. The fairy had trusted Cindy's coaching all this time. Now it was time for Cindy to trust Belinda.

CINDY SET both her favorite practice skates, as well as her performance skates, down on a seat in the ice skating arena. She'd arrived before Belinda, who was always surprisingly punctual, particularly for a fairy. The bus had been early, though.

The coolness of the rink helped Cindy center herself, the ice reminding her to be calm, focus on her routine. She'd worn all black and white that evening, black ski pants, white down jacket, black gloves and earmuffs. She'd considered wearing her bright red gloves, but that made her look too much like a TV serial killer.

Cindy looked down at the two pairs of skates: her practice set were made of bright white leather so her coach could watch her footwork better, the other, a deep plum color that would have matched her costume. She'd only worn them a couple of times to break them in. About a week after the accident she would have switched to them for all her rehearsals.

Maybe next year.

A soft white light appeared over her shoulder. Belinda had arrived.

"That's a pretty color," she said.

"Yes," Cindy agree, turning to look. "Sugarplum fairy colored," she said, teasing.

Belinda snorted at her. "Really?"

Cindy shrugged her shoulders. The costume had been

dramatic, a rich, dark color that would have shown up especially well on the ice, particularly with Cindy's light skin. She'd been told that she'd wear a wig for the event, something long and white with an intricate braid going down the back.

"Take the guards off your practice pair and untie them," Belinda said after studying the skates for a moment.

After Cindy complied, she looked back at her friend. Belinda's eyes had narrowed. The intensity of her stare felt like a sunbeam striking Cindy, chasing away the cold.

"Can I touch them?" Belinda asked after a bit.

"Sure," Cindy said. Belinda sounded strangely stiff and formal.

"No, can I *touch* them?" Belinda said. "You know. With magic."

"Uh, sure?" Cindy said. She wasn't exactly sure what the fairy was asking.

"Okay. Here goes nothing," Belinda said. She stared hard at Cindy's practice skates.

Bright blue-white light suddenly outlined Cindy's practice skates. First the right skate, then the left, slowly rose up and stood on the blade. They wobbled there for a moment.

Cindy found herself holding her breath. While it was one thing to watch Belinda perform, and to use her magic with her jumps and spins, it was something completely different to watch her skates suddenly take on a life of their own.

"Pick them up and put them on the ice," Belinda said, her voice sounding strained.

Cindy finally tore her gaze away from her skates to look at the fairy. Her natural glow burned extra bright, but not hot. No, her magic burned cold.

Weird. Yet another thing the TV shows had all wrong.

Cindy slipped forward, trying not to block the fairy's view of her skates. The skates themselves felt covered in ice. Her fingers tingled as they slipped under the magic spell. She lifted the skates and held them to the side as she carefully made her way to the ice.

As soon as Cindy set her skates down on the ice, they glided away as if a ghost had possessed them.

Then she frowned. No, it was as if they were doing her most recent routine, the one she'd been working on before the accident.

What the hell?

She glanced over her shoulder at Belinda, who gave her a great grin, showing off her pointed, sharp teeth.

"The skates still have a little memory of what you were practicing," Belinda said. "Because you rehearse so often, your practice skates remember a lot."

"Cool," Cindy said, turning back to stare at the skates performing on their own.

"Now comes the hard part," Belinda said.

Cindy gasped as a ghostly figure coalesced above the skates. It looked something like Cindy, but a more stylized version, like a line drawing.

A bright light appeared beside the illusion on the ice. Suddenly, Belinda was there, full-human sized. The ghost figure and the fairy danced together as the music of the fae filled the air.

Cindy's heart beat hard, as if she was doing all the work. Her leg muscles trembled through the arabesque. She found her arms half lifting for the spin.

She felt connected to the figure on the ice, somehow.

She concentrated on her form, lengthening her lines making her hands softer. The figure responded, appearing more graceful.

It was a beautiful routine. Belinda mainly mimicked

what the ghost figure did, except she added her own brilliant leaps and inhuman spins.

Cindy pressed her palms against her eyes to push out the tears that rested there as the routine came to an end. She wished she could hug Belinda, but all Cindy could say was, "Thank you. Thank you. Thank you."

Belinda nodded, then asked seriously, "Think that's brilliant enough for the officials?" She didn't look pale, exactly. Cindy could still tell that the routine had taken a lot out of Belinda.

"The officials would be idiots for not wanting to include that in the mid-winter jubilee," Cindy told her.

"They are adults," Belinda said sourly.

"True. I think they'll see how wonderfully magical it is," Cindy said. She paused, then said yet again, "Thank you. That was…I have no words to describe how beautiful that was."

"You felt it, didn't you?" Belinda said. "The magic. The routine. You were part of it, too."

"I did. But how? Humans don't have magic," Cindy said. While some humans were more sensitive than others, none had magic like the FBP.

"I think it's because you've been exposed to enough of my magic," Belinda said. "We've been working together and you know me. Better than some of my fairy friends."

Cindy bit her lip to keep it from trembling, then nodded. Skating had always been her primary focus. She had friends, sure, in school. She might, if tortured appropriately, even admit to her older sister being friend-like. But no one who shared her passion like Belinda, who worked as hard or strove so long. The other girls in the circuit were competitors, not friends.

"So let's do it again," Cindy said, her voice sounding

harsh. "There's that triple lutz in the middle section that needs to be cleaned up."

"You got it, coach," Belinda said with a grin. The fae music started up again.

Cindy focused harder on the two figures this time, pouring all her pent up emotions and energy into the ghostly skater, perfecting the routine.

It wasn't the same as performing. She would take what she could get while her leg healed.

The routine seemed easier for Belinda this time. She actually smiled a few times and seemed more at ease.

Maybe her heart was healing as well.

"STAY STILL!" Cindy told Belinda as she tried to attach the last purple streamer to Belinda's wings.

"I can't!" Belinda whined. She vibrated in place.

Cindy had at first felt honored that Belinda had asked her to help with her costume. But the fairy was so nervous it had turned into a game of "pin the streamer on the fairy". Even in the small green room that had been assigned to just the pair of them it had been difficult to catch up with the darting fairy.

"Just one more," Cindy said, as calmly as she could, reaching up cautiously to touch the top part of Belinda's left wing. The wing was stronger than it looked. Despite how it sparkled as though it had been covered in gold glitter, it felt like smooth plastic under Cindy's fingers.

They'd tried (and rejected) a bunch of different adhesives, including boob tape, finally settling on old-fashioned spirit gum.

Cindy quickly wiped a last brushful of the smelly,

sticky substance on Belinda's wing and attached the last streamer.

"There!" Cindy said, stepping back. "All done."

Belinda took off, darting to one corner of the green room then streaking across the ceiling to the other corner. The room was only big enough to hold two dressing tables, so it wasn't very wide.

"How do they look? How do they look?" Belinda asked, her voice squeaky with excitement.

"Great," Cindy told her truthfully. And Belinda did look wonderful. Her costume was a study in contrasts. One sleeve was white while the other was the same dark purple color as Cindy's performance skates. The skirt had purple and white stripes, and Belinda's tights were also one white, one colored, opposite to her arms. The plum color seemed richer than a human outfit, like it was actually made out of velvet, and the white parts sparkled with fairy magic.

Cindy wore black jeans (finally!) as her walking cast had just been removed the day before. Her blouse was also black, and she had a black scarf over her hair. She had darker makeup on as well, to help disguise the natural paleness of her skin.

She would appear as a shadow on the ice, a dark figure that everyone would ignore once Belinda started skating. It felt appropriate for their routine. Cindy's mom had teased her about being the power behind the throne. Cindy wasn't sure she liked being called that, however, she was also aware of how much power a coach had, now that she'd been coaching someone herself.

"Aren't you nervous?" Belinda asked, pausing for a moment in front of Cindy before taking off again.

"I'd run three laps around the arena if I could," Cindy admitted. She always had pre-performance jitters. She also knew that her physical therapist would *kill* her for straining her leg that way.

The door to the green room opened. "Two minutes," said the friendly stagehand.

Belinda froze in place. All the magic drained out of her. Cindy stared in fascination. Though the fairy still glowed, she appeared more angular and bony, as if she was made up out of sticks and twigs held together with the lightest coat of skin. Her costume grew plain and Cindy suddenly saw broad stitches along the side seams.

"You can do this," Cindy told Belinda. "Once the music starts, just let it flow over you. You've practiced enough it'll be easy. Trust me."

Belinda shook herself all over, like she was shaking off a sudden rain.

"And remember, this is just the first performance. You'll be great this time, and better next time, and the time after that," Cindy said.

Belinda gulped and nodded, all the magic flowing back into her, plumping her up (though she was still awfully skinny) and making her clothes look rich again. The fairy nodded again, then turned to Cindy. "You ready?"

Cindy couldn't help but smile at the impatient tone the fairy had adopted, as if Belinda had been the one waiting all along for Cindy.

"Ready," Cindy said.

She walked out of the room, a bright glowing ball of nervous energy at her side.

They walked down the darkened hallway to the side entrance of the ice as the crowd exploded with applause for the previous performers. Cindy felt the focused calm that always came immediately before a performance. She carried her practice skates instead of walking in them, which felt weird.

The previous performers streamed from the stage through the gate. The smell of their sweat and excitement mingled with the cold scent of the ice. Cindy nodded at them, relishing the shocked and surprised looks a couple of them threw at her.

In the program, only Belinda was listed. Cindy was just there as a coach. And she shouldn't be on the sidelines tonight.

They had no idea.

The lights stayed bright as Cindy cautiously stepped onto the ice. She was *not* going to fall and look like a dork. She held her skates high, the white leather covered in purple cloth that matched Belinda's outfit.

They walked to the center of the rink, the audience growing silent. They had no idea what to expect. No one had ever done anything like this before, even though the FBP had been around for ages.

Cautiously, Cindy put her skates down and stepped back.

The arena went black. The audience stirred restlessly for a moment.

A single spotlight hit the skates lying forlorn in the center of the rink.

The audience gasped as first one, then the other skate picked itself up, then gasped again as Belinda's magic filled in the shadowy figure who skated in them.

Fae music came trickling over the loudspeakers.

The performance began.

Cindy concentrated on the ghostly figure, ignoring everything else. She was aware of the officials sitting directly to the side. They weren't there as judges, not really. Still, Cindy knew she performed best to an audience and still found herself directing the performance that way, giving them the best view.

The routine went beautifully, with the audience gasping at the height of Belinda's jumps as well as clapping at the right times. Wild applause erupted as they finished. The number of roses and flowers thrown onto the ice was huge, bigger than Belinda's natural form. Cindy picked up a couple after grabbing her skates.

"Oh my goodness that was exciting! Don't you think that was exciting! Wow! The audience means everything!" Belinda said, burbling over as they walked back to the green room. During rehearsal, Belinda had always seemed slightly drained afterward. The energy of the crowd had fueled her this time.

"I know! I know!" Cindy said, wishing she could bounce along as she walked, but she knew she still had to take it easy on her bum leg. "It was amazing. You're amazing!"

An older fairy with the same golden brown skin as Belinda waited for them in the greenroom. She wore a sparkling white outfits that hurt Cindy's eyes.

Cindy turned to look at Belinda. "I can come back later," she offered.

"No need," the woman said. She gave the pair of them a glittering smile that looked like it hurt. "Thank you for helping my daughter," she said, bowing her head to Cindy. "I owe you one favor. You may call on Mrs. Marblewood when you're ready."

Cindy caught her breath. A fairy favor? She could ask for just about anything, she knew. That part the TV shows actually got right.

"As for you," Mrs. Marblewood said, turning toward Belinda, "that was fabulous! So ingenious! Your father would be so proud of you!"

Cindy had thought that Belinda had been a nervous

ball of energy before. Now, she physically shook. "Thanks, Mom," she said, her voice cracking.

They looked at each other expectantly, half a room of empty space separating them.

Cindy sighed. "Jeez," she said loudly, in her most bored teenage voice. "Go hug her already. I'll come back later."

Cindy was glad that she already had the greenroom door mostly shut before the blinding light of two fairies touching each other exploded.

No wonder the FBP didn't like touching mundanes. Not if when they touched each other it was, well, magical.

About a minute later, the door opened and Mrs. Marblewood flowed out of the room. "I'll be seeing you," she said.

Was that a promise? Or a threat? Or perhaps both? Cindy wasn't sure. It sure explained why Belinda made her uncomfortable sometimes, if she was emulating her mom.

"So what'd she say?" Cindy asked as soon as she came into the room. Belinda cruised from one corner to the next, not as nervous as she'd been before, but still flying high.

"She liked it! She really liked it!" Belinda crooned. "And she's going to help me find other fairies to compete against!"

"That's wonderful!" Cindy said, happy for her friend and yet at the same time, sad that Belinda would no longer need her as a coach.

Belinda came to hover just before Cindy. "She also said that our routine would be perfect for the next FBP-human alliance summit meeting. In Switzerland!"

Cindy gasped. She'd ever been to Europe, though she'd skated all over the US. "Really?"

Belinda nodded. "Really. And she really likes you. And

she wants to be our manager, and arrange for us to perform all over!"

"Wow," Cindy said. She knew that she'd go from competing to performing someday. She just hadn't expected it to happen so soon. She would get back to competing, though. Maybe next year.

Shyly, the fairy held out her hands to Cindy.

Cindy told herself not to shake as she reached out and touched the fairy's cold fingers. Uncomfortable fairy magic raced up her arms, making her shiver. Her heart beat wildly and she found herself panting.

They mutually let go after just a few moments. Cindy understood that Belinda had just shared something deeply personal: how the fairy truly felt at that moment.

"You really are that calm," Belinda said, her head tilted to one side as she looked at Cindy. "Weird."

Cindy chuckled. Then she paused, considering. "Do you want to keep the routine exactly as it is?" she asked slowly.

Belinda looked confused for a moment. "Of course!"

Cindy nodded. It didn't surprise her. Belinda liked doing all that magic and illusions. She wouldn't want to actually skate with Cindy.

"Only you'd be the one in your skates next time," Belinda added. "Dork."

"Dufus," Cindy countered. She knew it was a different path than what she'd originally intended for her skating career, skating with a fairy partner instead of competing on her own.

And maybe she'd get back in the circuit after a while.

But for now, the gold found in fairy wings would be better than any gold medal she could win.

THE PERFECT SHOES

PEDRO STUDIED Grandmother Maria's shoe closet mournfully.

It was three times the height of the wee brownie. Light-colored pine shelves covered all three walls. White will-o-the-wisps highlighted the corners and the lower area. Sparkling pixie dust floated through the air.

From bottom to top, the shoes were displayed to their best advantage: leather walking boots that were perfect for the indeterminate Seattle spring weather; glittering dancing shoes with kitten heels that would keep the wearer's feet feeling fresh all night; comfortable house slippers that encouraged long afternoons on the couch; the exact right shoe for every occasion, every weather, every whim.

The closet smelled of comforting leather and polish, with hints of sequins and carved wooden heels. Traces of cedar came from the shavings stashed in the corners of the shelves to keep away any miscreant moths, as well as the lavender-mint potpourri sachets Grandmother Maria made to keep all her ribbons and bows fresh.

Grandfather Alfonso had truly loved Grandmother Maria. He'd shown his love year after year by crafting the very best shoes for her. Only the tiniest bit of magic remained in his creations: the shoes were perfect because of his care and talent.

Pedro sighed again, the sound echoing in the tiny closet. He had to make something as equally amazing for his own true love, Isabella. But how? Particularly since Isabella had declared that she would marry the suitor who created the exact right shoe for her next week, on Valentine's Day.

Without meaning to, Pedro barred his teeth. His primary rival—that damn Miguel—made exceptionally fine shoes. His latest creation had *both* purple ruffles around the ankle as well as cute bows perfectly placed at the top of the shoes. Isabella had cooed over them and worn them all evening. Pedro's own creation—cute Mary Janes made from the softest, creamiest black leather—had barely rated a glance.

What was Pedro to do? Grandfather Alfonso had died that past winter (at a respectable 152) so he was no longer there to guide Pedro. Pedro's own father made merely adequate shoes at best. His mother always laughed at his father's efforts, saying that at least he was good at other things, a comment that frequently made his father blush.

Pedro despaired when he thought about his own shoemaking capabilities. While Grandfather Alfonso had always praised Pedro's efforts, he was afraid that his grandfather was just being kind, and that Pedro's abilities equaled his father's, instead.

Grandmother Maria was no help either. Pedro had asked her about his grandfather, how he'd always come up with such perfection. She'd merely blinked at him owlishly and said she didn't know. He'd just always seemed to know what was right.

Somebody must know the secret to making the exact right shoe. Though shoe making was a talent that all brownies were born with, some still made better shoes than others.

However…Maybe Pedro could go and ask the finest shoemaker in Seattle. Father Wilson. The grand priest of Celidrius, the god of shoes. The priest lived in a commune out in west Seattle.

When the FBP (fairies, brownies, pixies) had shown themselves to the humans back in the 1960s, demanding equal and civil rights along with everyone else, some humans had accepted them right away, before the all-race riots. The community-owned living space in Seattle was one of the oldest settlements of the FBP.

Very few brownies could afford Father Wilson's creations: his main trade was making shoes for humans. Not your everyday person, no, celebrities and performers. (Not politicians, however, Father Wilson was well known for despising all things political. He'd even refused to make shoes for the Queen of England.)

Would he talk with Pedro? Guide him in his own quest for making the perfect shoe?

He had to. Pedro would *make* him.

Pedro looked down at his own scruffy T-shirt and jeans. The shirt was his favorite, bright blue cotton emblazoned with a white-and silver picture of the lead singer from the fairy boy band NIMBY.

This would not do. Pedro must change into more formal wear. Not the robes and breeches of his parents, however. No, he would have to dress like a human celebrity. Hopefully, that would help Father Wilson see the importance of Pedro's request.

With a wave of his hand, Pedro changed his clothes. The stiff collar of his white, button-down shirt butted up against his neck. A creamy blue-silk ascot with the perfect Windsor knot flowed down his front, tucked neatly into his purple-and-gold paisley waistcoat. Black tuxedo pants with a shimmering silver stripe down the side flowed to his black formal shoes, which had been polished until they shone like mirrors.

He debated for a second adding a jacket, but decided that was too much. He wanted to appear rakishly charming, not like a waiter or groom. He mussed his short black hair (so it looked just like his favorite lead singer's) and glanced at himself in the full-length mirror that hung on the door to the closet.

He frowned. Something was not quite right.

His face held the sharp features of all his kind, though his nose was a bit smaller than most. Wide brown eyes that always appeared to be dreaming stared back at him. His skin held the dark appearance of a constant tan, like most of his family, showing their Hispanic roots.

Did he need the jacket? No. He remembered the famous quote from Coco Channel, about less is more. He dismissed the pearl stickpin from the ascot, as well as the gold chain linked from one pocket to the next of his waistcoat. For a moment, he shortened the pants to be the traditional brownie breeches, ending just below the knees.

Nope. That didn't work.

Something was still off, but Pedro decided he'd done the very best that he could. Maybe Father Wilson would help him with his wardrobe choices as well.

But now, Pedro was off to convince the high priest of shoes to teach him the secrets of the trade.

ONLY FAIRIES HAD wings they could use to fly with. Although, strictly speaking, fairies didn't really use their wings to get them airborne. Wings were more for gliding and guiding. Magic made them fly.

Brownies had their own powers, though, and magical ways of getting around.

As part of the pacts that humans signed with the FBP, they'd agreed to grow cabbage patches in various parts of their cities. In return, the brownies ensured that all animals used for meat, fur, and leather, produced the most amazing products. Plus, the brownies enforced humane treatment of the animals. The humans had been amazed at how economical the deal had turned out to be, with so much less waste as every part of every animal was used.

Pedro didn't understand why cabbage leaves worked best as portals for brownies. But all he had to do was to focus on where he wanted to go, step under one of the cabbage leaves in the garden in his own backyard, then take another step and be under the cabbage leaf of another garden, closer to where he wanted to go.

And he always knew where he was, whenever he stepped into a strange cabbage patch. It was something else all brownies were born with.

Since Pedro's family lived out in Kent, it took a couple of steps for him to get up to west Seattle. His first step took him into a garden in White Center. It was small, but hearty. A row of dried, bent-over corn stalks lined the edge. Rustling wind made the brown leaves sing softly. Kale continued to grow despite the cold. The rest of the ground lay bare, just waiting for spring.

The cabbage patch was protected from the Seattle winter by thin plastic sheets, held up with white PVC pipe bent into horseshoe shapes.

Pedro took a few moments to add some silver glitter to the PVC, making the hoops sparkle in the February sunshine. Then he glazed the plastic sheets, enhancing them so they'd catch more of the sun's rays.

Obviously, not many brownies passed this way, or the patch would be better protected. Pedro vowed to make a point of visiting more nearby cabbage patches to beautify them, once he'd successfully wooed Isabella. His darling wife should never be ashamed to travel anywhere her heart desired.

The next step took Pedro to the outskirts of west Seattle, close to the commune. He debated taking a third step, and actually landing in the center of the community-held garden, but he decided that would be rude. You didn't just show up in someone's backyard cabbage patch, not unless you knew the brownie well and had an open invitation.

Instead, Pedro tugged at his waistcoat, ran his fingers across the cool, smooth silk of his ascot, then darted off to the nearest shadow. No matter how bright the day or how dark the night was, brownies could always find shadows.

That afternoon didn't present much of a challenge, however: bright Seattle sunshine peered down out of a cloudless blue sky. Cold winds blew in from the Puget Sound carrying just a hint of warmer weather at the tail end. Trees were budding, and the bravest of flowers had already started poking their heads above the ground.

The community living space was two city blocks long, but only one deep. All the wooden houses faced inward, their backs to the rest of the world. To Pedro, they looked like the pictures he'd seen of English row houses, with wooden walls and dark shale roof. A huge community park and garden took up the center of the area, with a kid's fountain and splashing pool on one side, tennis courts on the other.

A tall, iron fence enclosed the space: leftover from the times when the community was at odds with the city and the rest of the world. Pedro hurried around the block to the opening on the far side.

These days, the gate to the area was never locked. Pedro doubted the rusted hinges on the huge fence even worked.

The park itself was full of old trees that had been there for close to one hundred years, twisted oaks and tall pines. A scattered collection of Japanese maples took up one corner, red buds cautiously waiting for spring. The food garden was to Pedro's left, close to the communal kitchen.

This was a proper garden. Pedro was impressed. Two

huge rosemary bushes guarded the entrance to the herb section. Tall sage plants bushed behind them. The parsley had been protected well enough to survive the winter outside, as had the thyme, marjoram, and oregano. They all shivered as the winds caressed them, carrying their sweet scents away.

Pedro hurried past them to the cabbage patch. It grew lush and full, sprouting huge cabbage leaves, not only green, but purple and gold as well. It smelled of rich dirt and felt like home.

Maybe some year Pedro's own garden could look as divine.

Pedro drew himself up to his full height (possibly all of five inches, as measured by the humans) and called out. "Father Wilson! I have need of your wise counsel. Please aid a young man in his quest for knowledge!"

Then Pedro placed the poor rejected Mary Janes that he'd made for Isabella on the flat stone in front of him. It wasn't a proper offering to Celidrius: traditionally just scraps of leather were used, or fanciful shoes that were created just for the god that even a brownie couldn't wear.

"I must learn the secret for making the perfect shoe!" Pedro declared. "I am desperate," he added softly. "Please hear my plea!"

Nothing...

Surely Father Wilson wouldn't ignore Pedro's call? Maybe the priest wasn't home? But the cabbage patch looked so lived in! So alive! Father Wilson must be in.

"Father Wilson!" Pedro called again. "Please guide me!"

"I'm coming, I'm coming," came a grumbling voice. The shoes disappeared from the stone. After just a few moments, a dark doorway appeared suddenly before Pedro. "Don't just stand there letting the cold in."

Pedro quickly scooted forward, stepping into the father's residence.

"It was just the perfect afternoon for a nap," the voice continued. "Now, close the door. Make me some tea. And we'll see what we have here."

Pedro quickly closed the dark wooden door, then blinked and looked around. He stood in a square entranceway. Cold white marble covered the floor. Huge silver archways—tall enough for a human—filled the other three walls. Will-o-the-wisps glowed in the corners. The air smelled stale, particularly after the rich garden. Blackness lay beyond two of the arches, while a soft, white mist covered the third.

With a shiver, Pedro changed his size to fit the vestibule so he no longer felt dwarfed by his surroundings. In the natural world, his size didn't matter. It was only in an artificial setting that he felt the need to change.

"To your left, you'll find the kitchen," came the voice, followed by what sounded like a yawn. "Make us both some tea. Then come join me."

Pedro opened his mouth to ask where the kitchen was, then glanced again at the arches. Must be through the arch on his left. It was the only one that seemed, well, open. He shrugged, then turned that way.

If he wanted to learn the secrets of making the perfect shoe, he was more than willing to start by making the most perfect cup of tea he could.

PEDRO FOUND a silver tea kettle waiting for him on the countertop. He ignored the cast iron pot, obviously for humans, sitting beside it. A human-type faucet stood over a large, round, brass sink in the corner. Pedro suspected that the faucet wasn't actually connected to the city's water supply, as the stream that flowed from it was mountain fresh and clean.

Pedro ignored the stove (probably also for humans) and set the pot to warm by running his palm across the front of it. Then he took a step back. He'd been so focused on the pot he'd not really looked around yet.

Cupboards made from dark oak stood above and below the brown-tiled countertop. An old-fashioned wooden icebox stood to his left, the human-style, black gas stove beside it, and the sink to the far right. More cupboards covered the wall to his right. A small table with two chairs were pushed up against the wall beyond the corner, next to an open doorway that led to a pantry.

Ah. There. Under the cupboards on his right were several wooden pegs jutting out of the wall. Large, small, and medium mugs hung there, made out of traditional brown clay. A few human porcelain coffee cups hung there as well.

A white teapot, painted with red roses and green stems, sat just below the mugs. A suspiciously well-used French Press for making coffee sat beside it. (Then again, this was Seattle. Pedro knew more than one brownie who actually *liked* coffee. No wonder Grandmother Maria complained bitterly about how the humans were corrupting the brownie youth.)

Above the collection of mugs and the teapot, Pedro smelled the bitterness of a fine English Breakfast tea. He opened the cupboard and wasn't surprised to see an entire collection of different types of tea. Most of it was stored in clean glass jars (unlabeled, of course) though there were a couple of boxes of human tea as well. The teas took up the entire bottom shelf, with a few more jars on the second shelf, at least two feet wide and just as deep.

Pedro stood, paralyzed by choice. What tea should he serve Father Wilson? Did he want something to wake him up? Or something soothing, so he could continue his nap? Did he want something traditional, made from dried dandelion leaves and spring flower petals, or did he want something human, made from coconut and rooibos?

How could Pedro possibly know? He had to choose, quickly and wisely.

He went with his first choice, that lovely English Breakfast that had called to him. It turned out to be a blend of human tea mixed with dried roots that would give the tea an earthy undertone favored by brownies.

While the tea steeped, Pedro found a tray and put two mugs on it. Then, because he was feeling bold, he also got out a plate and arranged some butter cookies he'd found, along with cream and honey.

Satisfied, Pedro picked up the tray and went back the way he'd come. Sure enough, in the hallway, a different tall arch now had a mist covering it, instead of being all black like it had been before.

Feeling more confident, Pedro stepped through, directly into what looked like Father Wilson's study. (The archways, he suspected, were like cabbage leaves: they didn't physically connect to anything, but were instead portals to whatever room Father Wilson desired.)

Father Wilson sat on a wooden shoemaker's stool in the corner, silently studying a shoe. In front of him stood a small table. It looked as though all the papers and sewing materials had just been shoved to the side. Father Wilson didn't bother looking up, but merely pointed at the table.

Pedro took the hint and placed the tray down, then silently poured the father his tea. He didn't presume to flavor it at all.

Then he paused, looking around. The father himself

wore a white shirt, just as pure as Pedro's, though he wore the collar open without a neck piece. His waistcoat was the blackest of black, with mere hints of silver that only caught the light when he moved. He wore the traditional breeches of the brownies that showed his knees, and his feet were bare.

White hair covered the father's head. It could be an illusion—brownies, like the fairies and the pixies, could give themselves any appearance. However, Pedro thought it probably was real. Father Wilson's face was long, the skin darker than Pedro's (though from the sun and not because it was naturally dark). Wrinkles ran the length of it, deeply carved around his mouth. The dark brown of his eyes had started to fade. His nose was short and spiked, though, like most brownies, and his chin and ears had sharp points.

Three long shelves covered with shoes ran from one corner of the room to the other. Antique human shoe forms stood in the far corner, the toes pointed every direction, as if they'd all been frozen in the middle of a frenzied dance. Strips of leather, ribbon, thread, and other finery hung from pegs beside the shoe forms. Books and tools covered shelves on the other walls.

Pedro took a deep breath, breathing in the comforting smells of polish and finery. He felt as though he'd finally found his feet. *This* was what he'd expected the office of the high priest of Celidrius to be like.

Looking around, Pedro didn't see another chair or stool. But that was all right. He comfortably lowered himself to the floor, automatically folding his legs into tailor's position, what the humans called "half lotus".

Father Wilson finally looked up. "Fine quality, here," he said, indicating the shoe.

Pedro realized that Father Wilson had been examining

the pair of Mary Janes that he'd left as an offering. He felt his cheeks grow red. The father thought those were good?

Pedro waited until the father had flavored his tea with honey, adding a dollop of cream, before he poured his own. The tea had the perfect amount of bitterness to it, so he only added a touch of cream before sitting back down.

The father now examined Pedro with the same care he'd taken with the shoes earlier. He had his head cocked to one side, as if curious about what he saw. "These shoes have no flaw," he said quietly, indicating the Mary Janes. "The stitching is perfectly even. The leather is as soft as any I've worked with. The proportions are exquisite, sure to make the wearer look cute, possibly even girly. These are wonderful shoes. Why do you think you need my help?"

Pedro felt his heart hammering. "What do you mean?" he asked as his brain scrambled to find the right words. "They can't be that good," he added.

"They are. These shoes are the finest quality," Father Wilson insisted.

"But—but—Isabella didn't like them! She rejected them!" Pedro said. How could they be any good?

"Ah," Father Wilson said, nodding. "The shoes are perfect, as they are. Just not right for your love. Is that it?"

Pedro nodded, still bewildered. Had he actually inherited Grandfather Alfonso's skill? And not his father's? He'd always assumed his shoes were subpar, based on Isabella's reaction to them.

"What does your love want in a shoe?" Father Wilson asked softly.

"I don't know," Pedro said. "Frilly bits? But she didn't like the lace slippers I made either!"

"Why don't you ask her?" Father Wilson said.

"Because, uhm, I shouldn't have to?" Grandfather Alfonso had always known what to make, how to create the perfect shoe for Grandmother Maria. He'd never had to ask. Had he?

Father Wilson smiled and shook his head. "It's all right to ask," he said. "It's like this tea," he added, lifting his mug. "You made a perfectly fine mug of tea. Wonderful, in fact. But you never asked me what I wanted. You could have, you know. Then you may have made the perfect tea for me."

Pedro blinked, surprised. The English Breakfast blend was very good. He could taste that. However, the father was right. Pedro had made the tea that *he'd* wanted. He still had no idea what tea Father Wilson might have desired.

"I'm sorry," Pedro said, starting to stand. "I can go make—"

"Sit down," Father Wilson commanded.

Pedro sat down again meekly.

"Now, this Isabella, how can you make her the perfect shoe unless you ask her what she wants?" Father Wilson said, driving the point home. "Unless you're living together, and you're not, are you?" he asked sternly.

Pedro blushed and shook his head frantically. They weren't living together. He didn't even know any brownies who'd flouted that tradition. It just didn't seem right, to live with your love without going through the rituals of sipping dew together from a midnight buttercup, of seeing each other at the dawn with all your friends and family witnessing it for the first time, of exchanging bits of leather, ribbon, and shoes as part of your vows.

"Then you have to talk with her," Father Wilson said gently. "Find out what her heart's desire is."

"What if it isn't me?" Pedro asked, speaking his truest fear.

Father Wilson shrugged. "Then it isn't you. You will be free to find your own true love."

It sounded so easy, but so complicated at the same time! He couldn't just come out and ask her, could he? That couldn't be right.

"You don't need my help with making shoes," Father Wilson added. "Or tea. You've made very fine examples of each. But neither is made on its own. They're to be shared. Learn to figure out what your partner wishes first."

Pedro nodded, still unsure. It sounded almost too human. Shouldn't a brownie, with magic, already be able to tell?

As if reading his mind, the father said, "Humans, now. They're easy to read. It doesn't take much to make a human the perfect pair of shoes. A brownie, though, is always surrounded by the perfect shoes, so they have to be specially made for him or her."

That made sense, actually. "All right," Pedro said. "I'll do it," he vowed.

Father Wilson blinked, surprised. "You're an odd mix," he said finally. "Based on your clothes, I didn't think you'd sit on the floor at my feet, like a true student would. You do want to learn. You just haven't figured out how."

Pedro nodded. He realized what was wrong with his outfit, finally.

It wasn't actually him.

No, what he should have done was wear the jacket and the pants with the T-shirt of his favorite band.

In an instant, he'd changed his appearance. He suddenly felt comfortable in his clothes, maybe even in his own skin for the first time in a long while.

Father Wilson beamed at him. "Much better!" he said. "Now, you are truly you. Go and find out what your love wants, and help her to be truly her."

"Thank you," Pedro said, bowing low from the waist. "You've given me much to think about."

"You're welcome," Father Wilson said. "I would offer you a position here, making shoes with me, but I suspect that isn't what you want, either."

Pedro blinked, stunned. "I…I beg your pardon?" he asked weakly.

"Your shoes show tremendous potential. Who did you watch as a young boy? Who showed you the art?" Father Wilson asked.

"My grandfather. Alfonso Rodriquez," Pedro said.

"Ah. Al's son. I should have known. But your future isn't in shoes, I'd wager," Father Wilson said. "Not if you don't see the value of these."

After Pedro left, he still wasn't sure what Father Wilson meant.

Not in shoes? But what was a brownie supposed to do if he didn't make shoes?

"WHAT DO I WANT?" Isabella asked, puzzled, finally sounding something other than bored. "What do you mean, what do I want?"

Pedro stubbornly stood in the middle of Isabella's living room. It was done "fairy style", the ceiling covered in pink and white blossoms, golden backless couches and chairs lining the living bamboo walls, and thick green grass covering the floor. He'd changed into the traditional brownie breeches and clogs, though he'd picked a bright orange T-shirt showing the logo of a human Mexican-food chain.

Isabella had reluctantly agreed to see him, though just for a minute. And only after Pedro had told her that he'd talked with Father Wilson.

"What do you want in terms of a shoe?" Pedro asked

again. "How can I make you the perfect pair if you don't tell me?"

"I shouldn't have to tell you," Isabella said frostily. She glared down her sharp nose at him, despite the fact that he was just a shade taller than she was. She looked magnificent in her rage, however. Her long black hair fell like a waterfall around her, like a great cloak protecting her. Brown eyes flashed with anger. Her wide lips, painted a very pretty pink, pouted at him.

"But how am I supposed to know?" Pedro said. "We're not living together, so I can't assume."

Isabella sniffed at him. "As if," she said, meanly. "My one true love would just know," she added after a moment.

"That isn't how it works," Pedro said. "At least according to Father Wilson," he added hastily as Isabella barred her teeth at him.

"What does he know? He's an old man. Why would you listen to him?" Isabella asked, as if she hadn't just been impressed by the fact that Pedro had gone to talk with him just a few minutes before.

"He knows the most about making shoes," Pedro insisted.

Isabella considered for a moment. "You do make adequate shoes," she finally admitted.

Pedro's heart leaped. Finally! He was getting through!

"But they aren't right for me," she added after a moment.

Crushed, Pedro hung his head.

Father Wilson had been right. But wrong, too.

Possibly Pedro's shoes were good enough, but he'd never be able to make the right pair for Isabella. Her heart was set on someone else.

Pedro could see that now.

"I hope he makes you happy," Pedro said after another

moment. While he suspected that he could have made Isabella happier, there wasn't anything he could do except to admit defeat.

"You…you aren't even going to compete?" Isabella said, sounding very surprised.

Pedro shrugged. He didn't see the point anymore.

"But I do like your shoes," Isabella said after a moment. "You make very good shoes."

Pedro nodded grimly. He wasn't even surprised that Isabella had only been interested in him for the quality of the footwear he made.

"Come see me after you're married," Pedro told her, pulling himself up to his full height. "I'll make you a pair of house slippers that will delight you."

"Nothing more?"

Pedro shook his head and took his leave.

Father Wilson had been right about that too.

Shoes weren't in his future either.

PEDRO STEPPED out from under the cabbage leaf at the mountain garden. Despite losing Isabella, he'd still made a point of visiting every nearby cabbage patch and beautifying them. He loved all the gardens he'd found, and he'd truly enjoyed making each and every one of them more magical.

This one had become one of his favorites. It was located way out east of Kent, out toward Sugarloaf Mountain. The garden itself was maintained by a local group of humans who grew food for those less fortunate in their community. Pedro had blessed the garden and made the crops produce even better than usual. (Fairies were all about the pretty flowers and lush grasses. They just didn't understand the practical nature of food, however. That took a brownie's touch.)

The cabbage patch was located in a greenhouse. It had been opened up for the summer so the delicate plants inside wouldn't cook. Pedro had taken the time to add will-o-the-wisps to the corners, so the greenhouse always shone brightly at night (something the fairies who came here to dance seemed to appreciate, based on the large fairy circle he'd found just past the garden, near the forest). Streamers of sparkling gauze kept the birds away from the cherries and grapes.

Pedro grew himself to half human-height, a comfortable form for him when working in a garden, his head coming up to about the waist of a tall man. The workers all knew him here, and greeted him with smiles and waves.

As Pedro made his way over to the far corner of the plot of land, intending to slip out of the garden and visit a nearby stream, a child detached herself from the group of humans and determinedly walked his direction.

"Hello," Pedro said, smiling at her as she came closer. It was so difficult to judge the age of humans, but if he had to guess, he'd say she was about eight. Her dark brown hair had been bleached lighter by the bright sunlight. She had a kind smile and fat cheeks, with hazel eyes. She wore a comfortable shift dress, made out of a colorful brown-and-orange cotton.

However, she wore the ugliest shoes, dirty plain canvas sneakers, with what had probably been nice bows at one point. They didn't fit her at all, were probably hand-me-downs from an older sibling.

"Hello," she said shyly. "What's your name?"

"Pedro," he said, still curious why she'd approached. "What's yours?"

"Anna Maria Gomez Marqueza," she said proudly. "But you can call me Anna."

"Nice to meet you Anna," Pedro said.

The girl giggled, but then grew silent, fidgeting, her fingers entangled in the hem of her dress.

"What do you want?" Pedro asked. It had grown surprisingly easy to say these things now, to ask what people wanted. Brownies, too.

"Do you make shoes for people?" she asked all in a rush.

"I can," Pedro told her solemnly. "What do you need?" He hoped she wouldn't ask for something similar to the crime-against-nature monstrosities that she was currently wearing.

"Something for school for the fall," Anna said. "Something…something nice."

Pedro had gotten very good at listening the last few months, and at hearing unspoken words. She wanted nice shoes so the boys in school wouldn't laugh at her, or tease her about her non-American heritage. She wanted so badly to be accepted for who she was, so that she wouldn't have to give up her heritage in this foreign place.

Even magical brownie shoes couldn't do all of that for her.

"I can't make you something for school," Pedro said.

The girl seemed crushed.

"I can make you something better for the fields, however," Pedro added, wanting to give the girl something. Maybe he could even talk her into handing him the shoes she was wearing so he could burn them.

Anna blinked, then nodded. "Thank you," she said. Then all her courage fled and she ran away, back to her mother and father waiting for her, standing on the edge of the group of other farmers.

Pedro smiled and waved, then turned and returned to his own quest of visiting the nearby stream.

The perfect shoes didn't exist, not for all the occasions in the world. Something that Grandfather Alfonso had never been able to teach him.

Only the perfect heart that tried every time.

INVITATION TO THE BALL

UNCOLLECTED ANTHOLOGY: ISSUE 19

JANICE FOUND NOT ONLY her hands shaking, but her brilliant white wings as well, as she picked up the golden envelop that had magically appeared just inside her door. Her name was inscribed across the front of it, done in flowing calligraphy, using the most expensive of fountain pens. The ink still carried a faint scent of cinnamon, and the paper felt rich and heavy as she ran her fingers across it.

Was this really an invitation to the royal fairy ball?

There were far too many fairies for everyone to be invited to each ball. Instead, a drawing was held each season. One hundred and one lucky commoners were randomly selected and sent invitations.

Was this truly her time? She was the right age, after all, having just turned sixteen.

Cautiously, Janice turned the envelop over. An actual wax blob sealed the lip—blood-red, with the impression of a crescent moon and stars stamped into it. The royal crest of the fairies.

Janice could no longer contain her excitement. She ripped the envelop in her haste to open it, drawing out the printed invitation and scanning the card.

Yes! The midsummer ball! In a week's time! And she was invited! Holy crap!

Janice couldn't help herself. She flew up and zoomed around her living room, bouncing like a rabid rubber ball against concrete. She raced back to the ceiling, which was covered in pink and red blossoms, then down, past the backless couches and chairs lining the living bamboo walls, springing up off the thick green grass covering the floor then around again.

Oh my goddess! What was she going to wear? How should she decorate her wings? Should she wear rainbow sparkles with yellow streamers? That had been the trend that spring. Did she have to wear formal fairy robes? That would be dull. Or should she wear something completely different and innovative?

What should she say if one of the princes asked her to dance? Everyone would be presented to the royal family during course of the ball. But what if she was singled out? What if she was to be The One?

Chosen to be The Queen of all Fairydom? Fairest of them all?

"Breathe, child," came a voice somewhere from far below her.

Janice glanced down. Her dowdy mother stood there, smoothing out the poor torn envelop, then clucking over the printed invitation.

Of course, her mother wasn't actually that dowdy. She was also a fairy, after all. But she was just so old-fashioned! She didn't understand the music that Janice listened to, or even like her favorite fairy boy-band NIMBY. Her mother never let glitter float behind her as she flew or left a trail of sparkling dew drops.

"I am breathing!" Janice said as she swooped across the ceiling again. "I'm just so excited!"

"I know, my dear," her mother said. "I remember my first invitation to a royal ball as well."

"Really?" Janice said. She dropped down to look her mother in the eye.

She had to admit, her mom did have kind of cool eyes. Instead of being golden or dark brown, like most of the fairies, her mother had blue colored irises. Her skin had a pink tint to it, which was more human than fairy, though Janice would never say that out loud, despite having been teased about it as a kid. And while Mom's hair wasn't truly red, it did have copper highlights to it that probably weren't part of a glamor.

Janice wore a modern jeans and T-shirt (yes, with the

lead singer of NIMBY on it. Duh.) Her own skin was more golden, like her dad's, and her hair was black and straight, though it did have red hues in bright sunlight. She hadn't gotten up the courage to actually dye it pink or green, though she threatened all the time, and had used various glamours on it to try out different colors.

Her mom was much more conventionally attired, though not in formal robes, still, a pretty blue shirt-dress with white buttons that went all the way up to her neck. At least her arms were bare, though underneath she wore white leggings. Her glittering white wings kinda sorta completed the outfit.

Okay. So maybe her mother didn't look completely dowdy. She looked like a *mom*, though, not a fashion model. Which was what Janice wanted to be some day.

This could be her chance. She could get *discovered,* not at the ball itself, but either before or afterward, at one of the fabulous parties.

"I was a little older than you when the invite came," Mom said. She looked off into the distance. "It was the midwinter ball. The whole palace had been coated in ice and glittered so beautifully. And the food they served! Golden honey mead in buttercups and delicate lavender crumb cakes that melted on my tongue." She gave a happy sigh.

"Who cares about the food or the palace?" Janice said. "What about the princes? And the parties?"

Mom gave a disapproving sniff. "They were there as well. Couldn't tell you much about the royals. They stayed on their side of the great fairy circle. I stayed on mine. As for the parties, well, we've had more raucous affairs here in the cul-de-sac."

Like many modern day fairies, Janice's family had a time-share agreement with the humans. In exchange for keeping the yards and surrounding area of their suburban neighborhood beautiful and lush, the fairies got to use the outdoor areas in the evenings and at night.

"But you were introduced, right?" Janice asked. "To the court?"

Mom nodded. "Huge long reception line that they rushed us through. Barely got a chance to say hello and do my curtsey."

"By the wings of the goddess! I'm going to have to practice my curtsey!" Janice exclaimed. She would also have to learn the latest dances so she wouldn't be awkward. As a fairy, she was naturally graceful. However, it wouldn't look good if she had to keep up a glamor the entire time instead of flowing with the music naturally.

"You'll be fine," Mom said. Then she looked at Janice sharply. "I know I can't ask you to calm down or not bounce off all the walls regularly before the ball. All I will say is that afterward, even if things don't go as you'd like, that you remember that something good comes out of every experience."

Janice rolled her eyes at that. Of course, her mom would say that. It was like one of a million cutesy saying that she seemed to roll out given any occasion. Like those human fortune cookies.

"Fine, I'll remember," Janice said, already forgetting. "Now, I need to go practice!"

"Practice what?" Mom called after Janice as she flew off to her own bedroom.

"Like…everything!" Janice called back.

Really, just everything. If her life was about to change forever, she had to be ready for it.

JANICE HAD PLACED mirrors along two walls of her bedroom, just so that she could be sure to see herself at every angle. It wouldn't do if she only presented as beautiful from the front. No, everyone one behind her as well as on either side had to marvel at her exquisiteness as well.

She had left the rest of her bedroom as plain as possible, so nothing would detract the eye from *her*. Her bed still lay in the center of the room, with a raspberry-sorbet-colored duvet cover made out of the softest spiderweb silk. She'd toned down the brilliant yellow of the walls to a more muted color, though still pretty and reminding her of the center of daisies. The desk opposite the walls was hardly used, as unlike the silly humans, all her homework from school involved magic and illusions and not writing and books.

Today, Janice had on a plain gray T-shirt artfully draped over one shoulder, while hanging off the other and showing her black bra, though bras were such a human thing and really, all Janice had was a bony chest and not much else. Her jeans were bleached blue denim and had been carefully torn out at both knees. She was barefoot of course—she wasn't a brownie with a shoe fetish, after all.

She'd done her makeup with a perfect smoky eye, just a hint of cherry on her lips, and bronze color highlighting her cheekbones. She'd practiced the glamor frequently until she'd gotten the look just right, copying one of the many human fashion magazines.

While there weren't many fairy models, the few that existed were famous one-name wonders. Everyone who paid any attention to modern culture (like, anyone who wasn't her parents) knew exactly who the fairy models were and didn't need it explained again and again.

The fairy models worked with human fashion

designers, generally as muses, though they could stomp the runway as good as any human model, the few times they were allowed to walk. The problem was that most of human cameras couldn't capture fairies in motion. It seemed that designers wanted their clothes to be seen and photographed at a fashion show, for some ridiculous reason. They could just wait until after the event and have an all fairy runway. Janice had heard of at least one designer who'd done that.

There wouldn't be any humans at the ball itself. That was for fairies only. However, there were both pre- as well as after-ball parties that famous humans would sometimes attend.

She just had to catch the eye of the right artist. She had cheekbones to die for, and she regularly practiced smiling with her eyes. Her runway walk was exquisite, though she sometimes wasn't sure what to do with her wings. Did she hold them out straight behind her? Let them kind of float and flow to the sides? The pictures she'd seen didn't tell her much.

Janice had also practiced her curtsey, sure that if it held just the right amount of grace and disdain necessary to capture the eye of a prince or two. There were at least half a dozen princes currently living at the palace, as well as an equal number of princesses. Not all of them were American. Frequently, they would only visit for a short while, then would go sit on foreign thrones. Royals frequently intermarried between the various families to keep the ties between all the groups of fairies strong.

The American queen was still considered young, being only sixty. (Sixty!) But those of royal blood rarely lived as long as the commoners, at least according to her mom, so the queen wasn't likely to make it much past seventy, unlike Janice, who could easily expect to live to twice that age. While the queen's heir had been chosen, the inheritance could always be challenged. And the queen might change her mind. She had before.

That was when things would get really interesting, at least according to Dad. Particularly if someone like Janice had managed to get herself married into the royal family at that point.

Janice put her hands on her waist and sashayed across her bedroom, catching glimpses of herself as she walked. No, that walk had too much sass. She was supposed to be serious as well as fabulous, not just fabulous.

A pinging noise interrupted Janice's contemplation. Did she want company? After a few moments of dithering, she finally accepted. Leticia, her best friend, popped into the room. She was dressed like Janice, in a T-shirt and jeans, though her shirt was obnoxiously orange and red and advertised a local Mexican restaurant chain.

"Oh my goddess! Are you still practicing?" Leticia asked, looking around at all the mirrors.

"Of course!" Janice replied. "Wouldn't you?" Really, sometimes she wondered why she was still friends with Leticia. The poor fairy had no drive, no ambition.

Leticia just shrugged. "I guess so. Maybe. But I don't expect to be *discovered*. Not like you."

Janice smiled. "I'm sure you'll find your prince, someday." It was a frequent refrain between the pair of them, that Janice would become a star, somehow, while Leticia would become the pride of her family, a jewel in her own right.

"So what do you think of this walk?" Janice asked, starting at the far corner of her room and walking seriously down one side and up the other. She held her wings out straight behind her this time, stomping like the best of the human models she'd ever watched.

"Seems too strict for the receiving line," Leticia said slowly.

Janice scowled, though that was exactly what she'd been afraid of. "How about this?" Janice asked, turning around and walking back the way she'd come. She still kept her wings straight out behind her, but she did try to soften her step.

"Better," Leticia said. "But really, you won't be able to just walk like that, will you? I mean, won't the hallway be crowded?"

"They'll make way for me," Janice assured her. "Part like the butterflies before a fairy ring." It was one of the neatest tricks that Janice had learned recently, to cast an illusion of butterflies in front of a pond or other special place, a distraction that humans had yet to pierce.

"Ohhh!" Leticia said. "Maybe you should have butterflies circling around you!"

Janice collapsed onto the bed beside her friend. "I'd thought of that. But Mom said no. Absolutely not." She sighed and rolled her eyes. "Evidently something like that might be used to hide an attack on the royalty or something."

"Are you kidding me? They're, like, immune to most magical attacks, right?" Leticia asked.

Janice waved her hand. "Butterflies. Pure distraction. Every time."

"Huh," Leticia said. "But they're so pretty! And graceful, right?"

"I know! Right? But Mom even showed me the instructions that specified absolutely no butterflies." Janice sighed again. "However, I can do this without too much glamor," she added her tone hardening. "I have the natural looks and drive to attract, well, anybody."

Or at least that was what Mom had told her often and

again. Janice had noticed that she was different than most of her friends, as she appeared to be the only one with much ambition beyond beautifying the local area and starting her own family.

Fairies just didn't have many artists mixed among them. That was much more of a human thing. It wasn't that fairies didn't feel things as deeply as the humans did. They did. But their feelings tended to be there and gone, melting away like dew on a bright summer day. Despite all the myths, fairies really didn't carry grudges for centuries. They'd much rather make beauty, not war.

It was why Janice so loved NIMBY. It was fairy music that actually made her *feel* things, emotions she didn't have names for. Mom didn't get it, of course. Leticia only sort of did.

Maybe someday Janice could meet the lead singer. Sit in on a jam session. Get the bad boy who led the group to look at her as something different and not just one of the hundreds of other groupies who surely swarmed him night and day.

She was the perfect muse for someone. She just had to be discovered.

"So what are you going to wear?" Leticia asked after Janice grew tired of strutting and refining her walk.

"You can't tell anyone," Janice said. She even found herself looking around the room, as if afraid that someone might have sneaked in and was now listening to them.

"Not a soul," Leticia said, her dark eyes big in her face. "Show me!"

"Well, I've considered this," Janice said. Her T-shirt and jeans transformed into a glittering gown. Janice had just learned the word *diaphanous* and thought it applied well to her dress. It was sheer and sparkling up top, with beautiful lines of crystals running from her neck down to her waist. Below, the skirt flowed out like an upside down flower. Her wings, which were normally a darker gold color, shone suddenly with white light. She'd even put streamers on the edges that floated delicately behind her, stirring with the slightest breeze.

Leticia looked at her critically. "It's a bit over the top," she said after a few moments.

"I know! That's what makes it perfect," Janice said. "Everyone will notice me."

Leticia just grimaced. "There's attention, and then there's attention," she pointed out. "Being on the worst dressed list isn't the honor you're really looking for, is it?"

Stung, Janice quickly changed. "Mom said it was too icy for the midsummer ball," she admitted she transformed her outfit. Instead of white and sparkling, now she was all yellow, with yellow streamers on her wings. The glittery top plunged down between her breasts, the V starting at her navel. Rows of shimmering gauze made up the skirt, flowing around her.

"It's pretty," Leticia said slowly.

"But?" Janice asked, hearing the unspoken word echo around the room.

"It's been done. There will be at least a dozen, if not more, other fairies dressed like that," Janice said.

"I know!" Janice wailed. She just wasn't good at coming up with new, cutting edge fashion. That wasn't her job as a muse, was it? No, the artist was just supposed to be inspired by *her*.

"Here, may I?" Leticia asked, coming to stand next to her friend.

Janice shrank down the glamor until she was just in T-shirt and jeans again. "Do your worst," she challenged her friend.

Leticia gave her a quick smile in the mirror, then

started carefully weaving her magic around Janice. It was just this side of being ticklish, as though cool spring breezes whisked across her bare skin.

The gray of Janice's T-shirt lightened up, turning stark white. Rhinestones bedazzled the front of it in a wavy, hypnotic pattern. It still hung off one of Janice's shoulders, the bra underneath a much darker, richer black.

Then Leticia worked on Janice's jeans, turning them from a faded blue to a faded black, a better counterpoint to the brightness of her top. The fringe around the torn out knees was now a brilliant white. Rhinestones studded the material around not only the front pockets but the rear ones as well.

The final touch was adding ribbons to Janice's wings. Instead of streamers, which were two to three inches wide, the ribbons were barely an inch across. They were made out of a shiny silver material that curled and fluffed, following the curves of Janice's wings.

Janice changed her makeup herself, making it more severe, with a much darker eye and a brighter lip, as well as highlighting her cheekbones even more. Then she punked out her hair, turning it several shades darker, shortening it and adding random spikes, making it stand up more.

When Leticia stepped back, Janice looked at herself critically in the mirror. She looked several years older than sixteen, at least when you discounted the bright white light that all teenagers glowed with. She was a study in contrasts, the dark jeans and white shirt, the hard makeup and soft ribbons.

"This is so perfect!" Janice exclaimed as she turned from side to side. "It's so, so…"

"You," Leticia said. "No one else would wear something like this. They couldn't."

"Is it formal enough?" Janice asked, knowing that would be the first thing her mother said.

"Here," Leticia said. A brilliant tiara now sat on Janice's head, formal and yet playful at the same time.

"Thank you," Janice said, catching her friend's eye in the mirror.

Leticia shrugged. "It was the least I could do."

"What do you mean?" Janice said. She saw the emotion welling up in her friend's eyes.

"You have such dreams," Leticia said. "Such passion. I just want to be a housewife."

"There's nothing wrong with that!" Janice said, though in her heart she knew she was lying.

"I know," Leticia said. "I'll never have to fight my way to myself, though. You will. Hopefully, something like this," she said, indicating Janice's appearance in the mirror, "will help."

Long after Leticia had left, Janice stayed in her bedroom, studying herself from every angle. Truly, Leticia had found the perfect outfit for her. It was modern, chic, fairy-like, and above all, fashionable.

Now, Janice just had to convince her parents that this outfit was the right thing for her to wear.

IT ACTUALLY DIDN'T TAKE TOO much to convince her parents that her outfit was perfect. However, they wouldn't allow her to wear the tiara. Evidently, it was in the *rules* or something, just like no butterflies.

What, were the royals afraid that the commoners might outshine them?

The before-ball party had been a bust. The tent had been depressingly empty, and the berry punch mediocre.

No one had stayed for long—they all hurried off to the ball itself. Plus, the only humans who'd been there had been desperate hanger-on-ers, not even D list celebrities. Seemed that it was only the after-ball party where things really happened.

The palace glowed particularly beautifully that evening, with magnificent pastel blues, greens, and pink lights sparkling on the earth-work ramparts. The building itself was grown out of majestic oaks, the trunks molded together on the ground floor, while a colorful hedge made up the roof. Fairy-cap mushrooms lined the path, brilliant red with white spots. Bubbles floated through the air, as graceful as butterflies but maybe not as pretty.

Guards inspected everyone's invitation before allowing them into the outer courtyard. Janice was suddenly glad that she'd listened to her parents. The poor young fairy in front of her (dressed all in yellow, of course) was sniveling that *she* should be allowed to wear her headpiece, that it wasn't a crown, not really.

Janice couldn't help but roll her eyes and step up to the next guard, showing him her invitation.

The guard gave her a cool, appraising look. Probably didn't approve of how fashionable she was. Then again, what could a fairy dressed in both formal robes with a touch of armor say? Poor guy probably didn't have much choice in what he got to wear.

He waved a wand over her head, settling her glamour firmly in place. She'd be stuck in this outfit while she was at the palace. Royals were just too damned paranoid. If she had come prepared with an after-party gown, she'd be able to change into that, but nothing else.

Janice stomped at least five feet along the path before catching up to the group of fairies in front of her, clustered around and all trying to get through the palace doors at once. Leticia had been right. It was really too crowded for Janice to be able to show off her model walk in here.

So Janice took her time, keeping her gaze cool. She tried to project an aura of disdain, meant to deflect the inevitable giggles from those fairies just too young to understand what Janice was.

How she was here to be *discovered.*

Still, she heard more than one whispered, snide comment about how she was in *jeans* and not a proper gown. One of the older fairies actually muttered something about how they'd have to add one more thing to the prohibited list.

Janice pretended not to care.

Just inside the palace door, the floor, walls, and even the domed ceiling of the grand hallway appeared to be made out of off-white porcelain tiles. Portraits of the royal family hung everywhere, in natural wood frames, some with moss still growing on them. The air held the heady scent of roses. The raucous noise of a hundred excited fairy conversations echoed off the hard surfaces.

Finally, Janice and the others pushed through the other end and into the grand ballroom itself. The room was circular, of course, and large enough to hold two hundred fairies, easily. Hundreds of mushrooms and toadstools dotted the floor, with the grand fairy circle in the center. Soft music wafted across the air, already enticing several fairies to start dancing.

A long line curved around to the left of the room. Janice eagerly joined it. She found it difficult to keep her feet on the ground, wanting to bounce along with the others.

This was the introduction line! She was about to be presented to the royals!

Janice tried to keep her cool. She found her back

straightening and her wings stretching out far behind her. As far as she could tell, most of the other fairies in the line seemed to fold up more on themselves as they neared the head of the line, while Janice expanded, taking up more room.

It was just one more way Janice would stand out. Especially amongst all the boring gowns and yellow dresses.

Finally, it was her turn!

Janice couldn't stomp forward. There really wasn't any room between her and the fairy in front of her. If only she could take more time to make an entrance!

She still smiled with her eyes as she stepped up to the group of half a dozen royals all seated on pretty pansies and violets. She performed the perfect curtsey, low enough to be respectful yet not bowing so far down as to appear obsequious.

When she glanced up, she realized that the royals were all chatting with each other. They were barely paying attention to anyone being presented. Plus, the queen of the fairies wasn't even there! It was just some of the princes and princesses, and not even the upper tier at that.

Janice bit her tongue so she wouldn't call out to the royals, draw their attention to those people in front of them. Wasn't it in their best interests to care about their people? Or at least pretend to care?

No wonder they didn't want butterflies or any other distraction! They were all too self-absorbed to notice what was going on around them.

With a huff, Janice stomped off, not joining the rest of the line that stretched to the food tables but strutting her stuff across the grand ballroom. She didn't cut through the fairy circle in the center—there was rude, and then there was unforgivable. She did make it to the opposite side of the room (where there weren't many others) then turned and glared at the royals.

Not that it was going to do much good. They wouldn't notice her. Not until she was *discovered* and they had to pay attention to her.

Janice vowed to make it her life goal to get re-invited to the palace. Just so she could snub them.

Warmed by her revenge, Janice softened her stance, determined to have a good time at the ball regardless.

JANICE STAYED ON THE SIDELINES, watching the couples and groups dance. When there were group numbers she danced with the rest of the fairies. That was her right. However, no one came up to talk with her or ask her to dance between times.

She sneered back appropriately when a group of fairies deliberately slowed down to stare at her, where she was standing with her back against the wall. They were all dressed in shades of pink and yellow, looking like delicate flower blossoms.

They didn't get it.

It surprised Janice that no one appeared to understand the statement she was making. How modern and fabulous that she looked, with her torn jeans and rhinestone encrusted shirt. How the silver ribbons on her wings completed the outfit, giving all the hardness a softer edge. How her short black hair gave her even more of an edge, particularly compared to all the flowing locks she saw around her.

It wasn't as if she could change her outfit, with how the guards had settled her look for her. No, she was kind of stuck wearing what she'd chosen. She wondered if maybe a gown would have been more appropriate for the ball, saving the fashion look for the after-ball parties.

"Excuse me," came a soft voice from the side.

Janice turned a cool look over toward the fairy beside her. He wore what would best be called a flouncy shirt, made out of off-white silk, with a collar that reached almost the edges of his shoulders. His vest was black velvet, with a beautiful pattern of leaves and vines embroidered in silver across it. His pants were a subtle green-brown, with just a hint of red around the cuffs. It was a modern take on an old fashioned outfit.

The fairy himself was older than Janice, though not as old as her parents. Maybe in his twenties. He had golden skin as well as black hair, and golden eyes.

"Yes?" Janice asked in her best put-upon voice.

"You seem…unhappy with the outfit you're wearing," the young man said.

"Whatever gave you that impression?" Janice said. "I'm just sorry that no one else in here had the guts to dress fashionably."

"Oh. I see," the young man said. "I, uhm, work here in the palace. I was going to offer to let you change outfits if you wanted to."

"Into what they're wearing?" Janice asked, waving a hand toward the nearest group of fairies. "Why would I do that? Why would I change so I could look merely ordinary?"

Even though that had been exactly what she'd been contemplating.

"Okay," the young man said, nodding, though it was clear he didn't understand in the least. "Just…if you change your mind, you only have to come find me. I'm Lorenzo."

Janice softened a bit. "Thank you for your offer. I'm sure it was well meant."

Lorenzo jerked his head over his shoulder. "Princess Arluanda told me to come and ask. I think you look fabulous."

He turned and rapidly flew away.

Huh. So one of the royals had noticed her. Janice suddenly wasn't sure if that was a good thing or not.

No matter. She'd made her entrance, as well as quite a splash at the midsummer ball.

And she was just going to have to live with that as well.

OF COURSE, the after-ball party turned out to be a bust as well. Though there were more humans around, and definitely some who Janice recognized from the gossip sites, there weren't any fashion designers.

She was just going to have to figure out how to meet one on her own.

Janice left the party early, flying wearily home. The sky was cloudy and gray, and a chill hung in the air. June-uary, as the locals called it. Not that fairies were really bothered by such things.

The night had been a bust as far as Janice was concerned. No prince had come to dance with her. No fashion designers had fallen in love with her. Just a lot of snooty fairies all looking down their noses at her.

Janice wasn't surprised that Mom was waiting up for her. Mom took one look at her and said, "Kitchen. Hot chocolate. Now."

Janice grinned, possibly the first real smile she'd had all evening. She drifted into the kitchen and waited while Mom bustled about, breaking off the sweetest corner of chocolate from the special bar they had, then filling cups with hot milk and melting the chocolate in them.

The kitchen seemed so homey to her. The floor was grass, of course, with little red toadstool chairs around a small, hand-carved wooden table in one corner. They didn't have a stove or oven—magic could heat up their foods better than any device. They did have a magically run refrigerator, for keeping things cool, as well as a huge pantry for herbs and ingredients.

Golden maple wood covered the walls and will-o-the-wisps glowed dimly in the corners as it was night. Mom's bright red teakettle sat on the green-tiled counter, the warmest spot in the room.

"Thanks," Janice said as Mom handed her the delicate green-leaf cup, wrapping her hands around the warmth and sipping at the sweet chocolate inside.

"Want to tell me about it?" Mom asked after a few moments.

"I don't know," Janice said. "No one was nice to me! No one even looked at me. One of the princesses actually sent a servant over to see if I wanted to change my outfit!"

"I see you didn't, though," Mom said.

Janice scoffed. "Not about to change and be *boring* and *ordinary* like the rest of them."

"Would you do it again? Go dressed to the ball like that?" Mom said. She held up her hand so Janice didn't reply immediately. "Seriously. Think about it. Would you do anything differently?"

Janice blinked and thought for a moment. "No," she said, shaking her head. "I wouldn't. Let them talk. Let them sneer at me. Just wait until I'm *discovered*."

Mom nodded thoughtfully. "I know, I know. You want a fashion designer to discover you, to be inspired by you. And maybe someday that will happen. Or it maybe it won't. Maybe some other artist will find you." She paused, sipped her own hot chocolate for a moment, before she continued. "Do you recall what I asked you to remember on the day you got the invitation?"

Janice bit her lips together. "Uhmmm…."

Mom gave her the brightest grin. "I told you that something good would come of tonight, even if your dreams weren't fulfilled."

Janice blinked. She wasn't sure what Mom was getting at. The evening had been a total bust.

"You see, while you might not have been discovered by someone else, I think that you've finally discovered who *you* are," Mom said. "*You* are also an artist. You won't conform to any standards, either fairy or human. It won't always be easy or comfortable. But you know now that you can do it."

"Oh," Janice said. That seemed huge to her. She'd always known that she was different than everyone else, at least on the inside.

And tonight, she'd shown everyone just how different she was. Not just on the inside, but on the outside as well.

"You'll always have a home here," Mom said softly. "A safe haven, from which to spread your wings and find your own way."

Janice nodded. "Thank, Mom," she said. She paused, then looked up.

Mom had already put down her cup and had opened her arms.

Fairies didn't normally touch anyone. It was just too painful to touch humans, to feel their lack of magic. With fairies, it was the opposite. Their magic combined and sparked together, frequently resulting in a supernova of light and energy.

Still, Janice could really use a hug right now. Mom's

magic was soft and warm and enveloped her, the light golden instead of bright white as it shone from the pair of them.

After a few moments, Janice pulled away. "And now, I need to figure out my next big statement."

Mom laughed. "Get some sleep first. And be prepared for more backlash among your friends and classmates. But yes, then you need to determine your next art project."

Janice grinned and hummed as she flew back to her room. Maybe it didn't matter that no one had *discovered* her yet. Maybe, as Mom said, she could just do her own art. Guerrilla theatre. Impromptu fashion shows. Installation pieces.

The world was hers to conquer. It just didn't know it yet.

FAIRY TRAPS

TERRANCE HATED the old fairy who lived next door—Old Fairy Smithers was what he called her. She was such a poor representative of the fairies in the subdivision! Just look at the garden she kept!

He kept the yard that his family time-shared with the humans lush and green. (Okay, so his parents helped. Fortunately, it was one of the chores they assigned him that he actually liked. Unlike cleaning his room, doing the dishes, or collecting dew drops for sipping.) He made sure that there were ferns and wild red cabbage, broad leafed bushes and rhododendrons, white corpse berry bushes that bloomed in the winter and heavenly pink and purple hydrangea that sprouted in the spring. He was lucky they lived in the pacific northwest, just outside of Seattle, and he could keep things green all year round.

Old Fairy Smithers' garden, on the other hand, was anything *but* lush. Her daffodils, crocuses, primroses, violets, pansies, and paperwhites were aligned in neat rows. Her flowers did have beautiful colors—he had to admit he really admired the fiery orange-red tulips that she grew—but they were *tame*. He'd bet that even the roses she grew had their thorns trimmed.

What was the point of being one of the fae if you never let loose in the garden?

Or for that matter, at any of the seasonal celebrations?

He'd never seen her dancing around the fire at any of the parties the fairies had in the subdivision. She certainly wouldn't show up to celebrate the spring equinox, which was just two days away.

The humans and the fae had come to an agreement after the All-Races riots in the 1960s, when the fairies, pixies, and brownies had joined the human civil rights movement and demanded that they be recognized as well. In exchange for keeping all the wild places clean and beautiful, the fae shared the spaces where they lived. Part of the pact meant that the fae kept lawns trimmed, gardens blooming, and maintained all the walking trails through the parks.

It also meant that on the nights the fae celebrated, the humans would stay safely locked in their houses from dusk until dawn, while the fae took over all the spaces outside.

Anyone caught sneaking around (usually human teenagers) were given a magic potion to make them sleep and forget everything they'd seen or heard.

For the coming spring equinox, there would be a huge bonfire at the end of every cul-de-sac in Terrance's subdivision and dancing until dawn. Multiple tables would be set up covered in food and drink. At the exact stroke of midnight, amazing fireworks would start shooting off.

When he'd been a kid, Terrance would gorge himself on the sweet honied crumb cakes and thimbles of milk and mead at all of the holiday parties. Now that he was an adult—well, almost, okay, so he was still just fifteen and wouldn't be considered an adult for another three years—Terrance was much more interested in flying hard above the flames, daring them to spark at him, as well as racing with his friends from one end of the subdivision to the other, challenging each other to feats of flight.

And maybe, just maybe, dancing with some of the girls this year.

But Old Fairy Smithers wouldn't be there, probably wouldn't be caught dead dancing topless beside the fires (unlike Terrance's mom), or shooting glittering fireworks into the dark sky (like his dad), or even sipping aged dew from a rose petal (he'd been told it was an acquired taste and he'd yet to acquire it—it just tasted like stale water to him).

No, Terrance would bet that the old lady would be

locked away under the earth in her fairy house, grumbling about the noise and kids these days. She'd yelled at him often enough for buzzing her garden. He hadn't even blown off any of the rose petals, barely stirred the leaves. Really.

She was just old. And she didn't understand about having a little fun.

Dusk had come and gone that evening and true night was encroaching. High clouds reflected the orange streetlights that the poor humans needed in order to see. (Those would also be turned off during the fae celebrations.) The air was soft yet brisk, another sign that spring was tumbling toward them.

Terrance was out in his garden, adding a couple of lemon-scented geraniums to the borders when he heard a soft cry, followed by a coo.

What in the world was that?

He flew up a short ways. He maintained his tiny fairy size, about twelve inches tall, with beautiful gossamer wings that had a tinge of blue. He didn't actually fly using the power of his wings—it was magic that kept him up—but he flapped them automatically and used them to steer.

He had no trouble seeing in the dark. His golden eyes made that easy. And his mom had insisted that he trim his black hair to keep it out of his eyes, though he really wanted to keep it long, like the lead singer in his favorite fairy boy band.

Nothing in *his* yard had made such a noise. He didn't see any stray cats, not that they would have been welcome. His people and cats just didn't get along, and the humans had learned early to keep their damned pets inside if they didn't want one of the fae to put a harness on it and take it for a ride, exhausting dear little Fido and leaving him half dead on their doorstep.

Terrance didn't hear the noise again, but something made him fly closer to the edge of the yard that his family shared with Old Fairy Smithers, then up above the lilac trees that grew there.

An oddly shaped box sat in the middle of her yard, a couple of feet across and tall, but it wasn't square. It had a soft peak in the center of it.

Terrance blinked his eyes and tried to peer closer. He gasped when he realized that there was some sort of magical glamor on the box that covered it in shadows, making it difficult for him to see it. Goosebumps ran across his chestnut colored skin, maybe even making it a shade more pale.

He knew he wasn't supposed to cross over the property line, to go into Mrs. Smithers' yard. His parents had told him that he'd be grounded for a week the next time he did.

But something was hinky over there! Surely his parents would understand that.

The night breezes carried a soft giggle over the lilac trees.

That sounded suspiciously human.

However, humans didn't have magic, not really, and particularly not the kind that was strong enough to hide their appearance from one of the fae.

Terrance flew back and forth on his side of the lilacs for a few moments, agitated. He wasn't supposed to go over there. He knew it. He knew the consequences.

Someone had to, though.

With a determined flit, Terrance flew over the tops of the lilacs and into Old Fairy Smithers' yard.

Instantly, the odd shaped box in the center of the yard was clear.

It was a baby! A human baby! In one of those carriers they had to protect their young. Terrance thought it might be called a car seat, but he wasn't sure. Fairies didn't drive cars, didn't need them—they could just fly or use magic to get wherever they needed to go.

Terrance flew over to the baby. Stupid thing grabbed at him with its chubby hands. He probably just appeared as a shiny golden light to it.

It had rosy cheeks and pale white skin. It tracked his movements with wide, blue-gray eyes. Soft wisps of red-gold hair covered its head. Black belts kept it strapped into the carrier, probably so it wouldn't get into any mischief. It smelled of sweet milk and some sort of perfume that the humans used.

It kicked with its fat legs and waved its arms, then giggled again.

At least it was a happy baby and not screaming at the top of its lungs, unlike the babies he'd read about in the latest *Encounters* magazine, which was filled with fictional accounts of human-fairy interactions, many of them lurid or impossible.

But what was a baby doing here? Why did Old Fairy Smithers have a child, a *human* child, in the middle of her pristine backyard? Nestled neatly between the purple hyacinths and the creeping red sedum?

The humans were going to *freak* when they found out. In the olden days, sure, a fairy might snatch a baby and leave a changeling in its place. It would be years before the humans would miss it, and the fairies would have gotten their entertainment out of the kid in the meanwhile.

Sometimes the human children would be sent back to their parents to work as ambassadors between the humans and the fairies. Frequently, they would grow up to become famous courtiers, kings, or queens. Humans hadn't seemed to mind that too much.

Of course, all they remembered was that their precious child had been taken.

The fae had agreed to stop stealing children as part of the pacts. (Not that they really were doing it that much anymore. It was easy enough to find places to watch kids from.)

If Old Fairy Smithers had actually taken a child… Terrance shivered at the thought of the consequences she would be facing.

Determined, he lighted on the handle that had made the box such an odd shape when it was merely shadows. He changed his size, growing slightly bigger, so that he could at least wrap his hands around the handle.

However, try as he might, he couldn't lift the damned thing. It was just too heavy.

Terrance struggled, breaking into a sweat that instantly chilled in the night air. The carrier was heavier than any boulder, that was for damned sure. But he should be able to use his magic to lift it, right?

He flew from side to side, anxious and confused. He could lift rocks that were the size of this carrier in his garden. He should be able to pick up the damned things.

Although… Maybe he couldn't lift it because it wasn't a natural thing, but rather, was man-made.

He remembered reading about an entire village that banded together in order to steal a baby once. None of them had been strong enough to lift it and its cradle on their own.

Damn it! How had Old Fairy Smithers managed to get this thing here? She must be a *lot* stronger than she looked. Then again, she was ancient. The powers of the fae did increase as they aged.

"Don't worry," Terrence said, talking softly to the kid. "I'll go get help."

The child seemed more fascinated with the foot that it had just managed to catch in its hand than with the tiny golden light floating above it.

At least it wasn't too cold, despite the fact that the thing was in merely a T-shirt and shorts, as well as cute booties with pink lace around the tops.

"I'll be right back," Terrance promised, then he raced back to his own yard, diving below the grass and into the fairy house underneath.

Surely his parents would understand. They had to!

Old Fairy Smithers wasn't just a danger to the neighborhood, but to all the fairies.

She had to be stopped.

"NOW, what did we tell you about going into Mrs. Smithers' yard?" Mom asked, her arms across her chest, her glare angry enough that Terrance could almost feel real heat coming from it.

They stood in the living room, with Dad still sitting on the backless sofa leafing through one of his books of poetry. Mom stood on one side of the sofa, while Terrance confronted her from the other side. He figured it was better that way—maybe she wouldn't just smack him for being disobedient.

Thick green grass covered the floor, springing back immediately even when Terrance stomped on it. Pretty pink, lilac, and white poms covered the ceiling. The petals had stirred slightly when Terrance had raced into the room, but now they were still again. The yellow centers of the flowers glowed softly, lighting the brightly colored backless furniture and softly scenting the air.

The setting was far too peaceful for the rage and terror that filled Terrance.

"Look, Mom, I know! All right? I know. But there's a baby over there!" Terrance explained. Again.

Why didn't his parents believe him? All they had to do was fly outside and take a look! It wasn't as if they couldn't magically change out of their indoor, kind of drab clothing into something more appropriate for being outside at night. He'd seen his mom change from frumpy to glamourous with the wave of a hand, and Dad tried hard to never be outdone by his wife.

"Why would Mrs. Smithers have a baby in her backyard?" Dad asked reasonably, setting his musty old book carefully to the side.

"I don't know," Terrance said. "She's ancient. Maybe she was so old that she's forgotten about the human-fairy pacts."

"She's not that old," Mom countered.

"She sure seems ancient," Terrance said. "What?" he asked when his father stood up beside his mom, facing him.

"Terry—" his dad started.

"Terrance," he automatically corrected. He wasn't a kid anymore.

"Fine. Terrance," Dad said. "I'm sure that we seem ancient to you as well."

Terrance knew better than to agree with that. Calling his mom and dad old would probably add another week to his grounding.

"Mrs. Smithers has just had a hard life. Her husband was killed in a tragic airplane accident. Her sons have died, as well," Dad said.

Huh. Terrance hadn't known any of that. He'd assumed

that she'd never had any kids as she didn't seem to understand him at all.

"She's talked about coming to one of the celebrations this year," Dad continued. "That she can finally put the mourning away."

Terrance tried hard not to roll his eyes. Fairies didn't *mourn*, not like the humans did, wallowing in their tragedies. That just wasn't done. There were too many bright and beautiful things in the world to get caught up in sadness.

Now, anger, or revenge, that he understood. Though again, all of the fae tended to be mercurial, raging one minute and laughing the next.

"But that still doesn't explain why there's a human baby in her yard!" Terrance countered. "I feel sorry for her. I do. But she's gone crazy if she's kidnapping humans."

Dad and Mom exchanged a look. Terrance had gotten better at reading those silent communications as he'd grown older. This one clearly said that they needed to humor him, despite what they "knew" to be the truth. It reminded him of the one time when he'd been a kid and he'd had nightmares about red-eyed monsters hiding in the shadows, until Dad taught him how to rage and pretend to be a monster himself.

"I'll come with you," Dad said. "And if there *is* something there, I'll report it to the HOA."

That made Terrance blink in surprise. He hadn't thought about who they'd contact if there was a baby, just that they had to save it.

Contacting the Home Owner's Association was a serious step. Everyone had to abide by their rules, human and fairy alike. His parents had encouraged him to go to the youth meetings, but it had all seemed far too stuffy and formal.

"Thanks," Terrance said. He meant it.

Hopefully, Mrs. Smithers hadn't done anything too crazy with the baby yet.

OF COURSE, the baby was long gone by the time Terrance and his dad flew into the backyard.

They stayed on their side of the lilacs, flitting back and forth, peering over the trees.

"It was there, Dad, I swear it was," Terrance said. He was in deep shit now, and he knew it.

"Mmm hmmm," Dad said, his lips pressed together in a firm line of anger.

"I wouldn't make something like that up!" Terrance argued. "Why would I? Particularly since I know I'm not supposed to go into Old, I mean, Mrs. Smithers' yard?"

"True," Dad said, slightly mollified. He lifted his nose to the air and sniffed, suddenly growing very still, hovering stiffly.

"What is it?" Terrance whispered, afraid to speak any louder.

Dad ignored him. He suddenly flew to the far edge of the lilacs. The trees were a couple of feet thick. Even though they grew only on the human property that Terrance and his family maintained, he'd always considered the middle of them to be the border between the two yards.

Finally, Dad turned to Terrance. "Can you smell that?" he asked quietly.

Terrance flew up beside his dad and hoovered there, sniffing the air. All he smelled was good dirt, the sweetness of the hyacinth, the powdery, sour smell of the daffodils and tulips. He shook his head. He didn't smell anything that wasn't natural.

Dad just nodded. "You're young yet," was all he said before he turned and flew back toward their own house.

"What was it? What did you think you smelled?" Terrance said, racing up and stopping his dad before he could pop down below the ground and into their fairy house again. Had he smelled the baby, maybe?

"There was the remnants of an enchantment spell," Dad said slowly. "Which makes sense, that some of a spell should remain, if it was strong enough to fool you."

"What sort of enchantment?" Terrance said. Weren't those sorts of spells generally done to take something that was mundane and make it magical? Surely Old Fairy Smithers wasn't trying to give magic to a human! If that was even possible.

"I don't know," Dad said. He shrugged, his golden wings bobbing. "I do think you saw something."

Terrance's wings sagged with relief. "Thanks, Dad," he said. He meant it.

"But we don't have enough to take to the HOA," Dad continued. He looked over his shoulder, in the direction of Old Fairy Smithers' yard. "We're just going to have to keep an eye out, see what else we see."

Terrance glance back as well. The lilacs blocked all view of the prissy yard back that way. He'd follow his parents' rules and wouldn't go into Old Fairy Smithers' yard.

However, he would keep an eye on her, and whatever games she was playing.

LUCKILY, neither Mom or Dad decided to ground Terrance for flying into Mrs. Smithers' yard. He did volunteer for more yardwork, however. There would be some pre-spring equinox parties, and he wanted to make sure that their yard was even more beautiful than anyone else's.

Of course, his parents suspected he had an ulterior motive—by working in the yard, he'd have a much better opportunity to keep an eye on Old Fairy Smithers'. His parents were happy to accept his offer, though, as long as he stayed on their property.

He didn't reply that they didn't need to order him around like a stupid dog, like in those cartoons where the humans shouted at the top of their lungs for their pet to, "STAY!"

He might have said, "Woof" under his breath once or twice, however.

That morning, Terrance searched the news for reports of a missing kid. However, no one reported their baby being stolen.

Had they not noticed? Was there a changeling in its place? That would explain the lack of panic and alerts.

He still didn't understand why Old Fairy Smithers might take a child in the first place.

Terrance didn't have any lessons that day. Fairies didn't really go to school, not like human children. Instead, they had individual lessons in magic, flying, potions, illusions, like that. Terrance could take as many lessons as he wanted, at his own pace, as long as he regularly went.

The adults seemed to understand that nothing would get learned either a couple of days before as well as a couple of days after a large celebration.

Instead, Terrance got up midmorning and went out into the garden. He finished planting the scented geraniums, then brushed their leaves with his fingertips, scenting the nearby air.

Building a garden took more skill than Terrance had

originally thought. Not only did he have to bring a harmonious (but still wild) shape to the garden, with all the levels, he also had to make sure that neither the colors or the scents clashed. He felt as though he was getting the hang of it, finally, after that first summer with the disastrous maples that hid all the roses.

Humans asked their children all the time what they wanted to be when they grew up. Fortunately, fairy adults didn't make that mistake. Children would choose their path when it was revealed to them. Even though Terrance wanted to rush ahead and make the declaration that he was going to become a master gardener, he didn't state his intention. Not yet. Not until he was actually sure. He didn't want to be like that old man in the stories who'd chosen the wrong path and then was too stubborn to choose again when he'd realized he'd made a mistake.

The yard next to the human house was composed of the perfect combination of grasses to ensure that both the sunny parts as well as the shaded areas stayed green. Terrance trimmed it once a week, buzzing over it with his magic to keep it short and healthy. He was lucky in that he really only had to water it during the summer.

Outside of that little square of grass, however, was what Terrance considered *his* territory. The lawn was enclosed on all sides with other plants, the lilacs on the western side, roses and camellias to hide the wooden fence on the east, and a tiered wildness to the north that butted up onto the park that circled the subdivision. (He'd always felt sorry for those poor fairies who only had a yard to play with, that was surrounded on all sides by houses.)

A trail through the park lay several yards past the trees. Terrance kept his portion of the path well maintained so the humans could walk undeterred by roots, branches, or bramble. On either side, though, he encouraged the wildness of the woods to take hold, so the humans wouldn't even think to stray from the path built for them. Thus he ensured the privacy of the yard his family shared with the humans.

Terrance had several rock flowers tumbling down the front tier, as well as some wild oregano (that would take over everything given a chance). He was trimming those back when he heard the same call he'd heard before, that soft giggle and coo.

Damn it! The baby was back!

But it wasn't coming from Old Fairy Smithers' yard this time. No, now it was coming from directly in front of him.

The baby was now in the woods?

Who would abandon a baby there? There was something not right going on.

Plus, Dad had said it was some sort of enchantment spell going on.

Terrance flew up further then hoovered, listening hard.

Yes, there. Through the trees. He thought he saw the dark box that held the baby, sitting in the middle of the trail.

It didn't occur to him until much later that he shouldn't have been able to see anything through the bramble and bushes and trees.

Terrance flew directly toward the noise. The dark shadows dissolved again as he drew near, showing the same baby in the same car seat.

At least the baby still looked happy and healthy. It kicked in its seat, legs splayed and arms flailing, as if it was play-fighting with something.

When faced with the baby under the trees, Terrance had more of an understanding why fairies were always attracted to babies. There was a simple magic to its giggles and its coos, the subtle sweetness of its milky breath drawing him closer.

He knew, however, that babies didn't stay babies forever. Once it stopped being cute, he'd send it back to its human family

The path the car seat sat on was plain dirt, tinted a lighter brown than regular earth to make it obvious for the poor, oblivious humans. Terrance flew a couple feet up the path, staring at the ground, trying to see who would have walked there, carrying a baby.

For a moment, he thought he saw cloven hooves, as if a goat had passed by.

No one in the neighborhood had goats. He was certain of that. No one would be walking a goat either, not in this part of the trail. Sure, there may be people with pet goats in the city of Seattle. He would bet the weirdos up in Fremont might do that. But not here in his nice, cozy subdivision.

Terrance shook his head and rubbed his eyes, then peered at the ground again.

Now, he thought he saw the splayed toes of an overly large bird.

What, had some idiotic stork taken it into his head that he was actually supposed to deliver babies to humans? Complete with car seat? No, that was right either.

Terrance touched down on the dirt of the trail and closed his eyes. He felt the solid earth under his feet supporting him, could feel the paths of worms and beetles sliding along underground. The smell of fertile soil rose up, along with the sweetness of blackberries from the bramble and the musty scent of the decaying leaves and pine needles. He heard the breezes playing with the tops of the trees and the far away swish of traffic on the interstate a few miles away. He could still taste the sweet honey cake crumbs he'd had for breakfast, that seemed to mingle with the milky smell of the baby.

When Terrance opened his eyes, instead of a bird track, he saw the splayed bare feet of a creature with unnaturally long toes.

The cackle he heard behind him made him turn around and fly up, ready to disappear if something was actually threatening him.

Instead of a human baby in the car seat, he saw a pixie, grown to the size of a child. The pixie—he thought it was a girl—had bright red, straw-like hair that stuck out from her flattened face and around her pointed ears. An overly wide smile grinned at him, showing him pointed, crooked teeth that looked about as sharp as his own. The eyes were huge in her face, particularly compared to humans, fairies, or brownies, with very little white around the brown and green flecked irises, making her look more like an animal, or a horse, the traditionally favored ride of the pixies.

"Ah, you can see me," the pixie said, sounding as disappointed as a three-year-old when told it was time to go to bed.

"I can," Terrance said, unsure if he should stay or run away. "Who are you?"

"I'm Annin," she said. She stayed where she was, strapped into the seat, her stick-like legs and feet flopping.

"Why are you pretending to be a human baby?" he asked.

Annin rolled her eyes. "Some of the humans don't believe that the fairies will uphold their end of the pact, and that they've fallen back into their old ways of stealing babies."

"Why would we do that?" Terrance asked, confused.

"Admit it. You thought that baby was pretty danged cute," Annin said. "You tried to lift the car seat that first night." She transformed momentarily back into the baby again.

The smell of sweet milk and perfume rolled over Terrance. He shook his head and glared at her until the glamor faded.

"I was trying to save the baby from Old Fairy Smithers!" Terrance protested. "I wasn't trying to steal the thing. Besides, where would I keep it? My parents would throw a fit. And they'd report me to the HOA." He couldn't help the shiver he gave at the mention of them.

"True," Annin said, nodding. She sighed. "I've been doing this gig for half a year now, and haven't tempted a single fairy."

"Maybe you need to find something else to do," Terrance said, maybe a little angry at having been taken in by her disguise.

Annin thought for a moment, then she grinned. "Naw. It's too much fun pretending to be a baby and fooling the fairies, even if it's only for a little while. You won't tell anybody, will you?"

Terrance opened his mouth, then shut it again. "I have to tell my parents," he said.

Were those tears in Annin's eyes? She certainly looked that heart broken.

"But I won't tell anyone else," Terrance said. "I promise."

Immediately, Annin cheered up. "Great!" she said. "See you around!" she added as she disappeared with a poetic soft pop, followed by what sounded suspiciously like a kid blowing a raspberry.

Terrance sighed, nodding to himself. At least that cleared up why he thought there was a baby.

Were fairies really stealing babies? Leaving changelings in their place? There wasn't any need for that sort of thing, though. Not these days. If the fairies really wanted contact with people, all they had to do was go live in one of the cities. Not a fate he'd wish on anyone, quite frankly.

Slowly, Terrance flew back into his yard. It would have been much more cool if Old Fairy Smithers had actually stolen a child. Then he could claim that he'd stopped her.

Speaking of which…Old Fairy Smithers was out in her yard tending to her flowers.

When she saw him, she beckoned for him to come over.

Terrance froze for a moment. Of course, his parents wouldn't yell at him if she invited him over, right?

Wondering if this might be yet a different type of fairy trap, Terrance flew over the lilac trees and into Old Fairy Smithers' yard.

She seemed ancient to him. Her face was round as an apple, her skin the gray of dried driftwood, covered over in wrinkles. Beady black eyes stared daggers at him from on top of a sharp nose. Her lips were pressed firmly together in a line of disapproval.

Had she seen him the night before? Was she going to take an inch off his hide as well?

But then the ancient crone smiled. Though the wrinkles around her eyes and mouth multiplied, she still oddly seemed younger. Her teeth were still white and sharp and looked capable of taking a bite out of an unripe strawberry. She wore a pretty enough sunbonnet woven out of bright yellow straw. Her shirt looked old-fashioned—high necked and long sleeved—made out of white cotton with tiny purple violets printed on it. She wore pants like Mom did when she was working in the garden, woven from thick cloth with extra padding in the knees.

"Heard you talking with the pixie," Old Fairy Smithers stated simply.

Terrance gave her a tentative nod. It wasn't technically breaking his promise if someone had seen him and Annin together, right?

"I'd wondered why a baby had appeared in my backyard," Old Fairy Smithers' said, nodding. "Glad to know it was a pixie and not you who'd put it there."

"Why would I put a baby in your backyard?" Terrance asked, completely confused now.

She gave him a sharp look, then she sighed. "I lost my boys, you know."

Terrance shook his head. Alright, so he kind of knew, but didn't, not really.

"I'd had twins," she said softly.

Terrance felt his eyes grow wide. Fairy twins were rare, so much rarer than human twins.

However, there were also so many stories about how one twin would turn evil.

Old Fairy Smithers nodded, as if she could hear what he was thinking. "Egfrid wasn't a bad boy."

Terrance didn't remark on how, with a name like that, he could have been *good.*

"But he was the more wild of the two. Always daring his brother Edward to do bigger, crazier stunts," the old fairy continued. "He honestly thought he could survive jumping down a wild, surging waterfall, onto the rocks below. But he told Edward to do it first."

She sighed. Suddenly her age returned, and she looked as ancient as Terrance had always believed her to be.

"Edgrif was a good enough boy that he came back and told me about it. But he didn't stay. He went back to the same waterfall, as if to prove to himself that he could have done it, and he lost his life, same as his brother did."

Old Fairy Smithers sighed.

Terrance felt as though the bright spring sunshine had just been blotted out by a dark cloud. He could smell the grief and rage wafting from the old lady, like the smell of ozone from a thunderstorm. Cold winds brushed against his neck, warning of the coming deluge. His mouth dried out and he held himself ready to disappear.

The old fairy shook her head, and the storm dissipated. She made herself look up and plastered a smile on her face, one that Terrance could tell was obviously fake.

But at least she was trying.

"Edward died during the spring equinox," she said after a few more moments. "Egfrid died during the summer solstice. And the year before that, my dear husband, Mr. Smithers, was killed on the winter solstice."

Terrance couldn't help but shiver. No wonder Old Lady…no, Mrs. Smithers, didn't celebrate the fairy holidays!

"I'm sorry," Terrance said. "That must have sucked."

For a moment, Mrs. Smithers looked offended. Then she gave a great snort of laughter. "Yes, indeed, it really has sucked." She smiled at him, and the sun came out again, beaming down warmly on Terrance's head.

"I will make it to the spring equinox this year," she said, sounding determined.

"I'll dance with you if you do," Terrance offered.

Then he shook himself. What the heck was he doing? Offering to dance with an old fairy? His friends were all going to make fun of him, that was for danged sure.

"Who could pass up such a gallant offer?" Mrs. Smithers said. Some pink returned to her cheeks, as if she could suddenly feel the sunshine as well. "I will hold you to that, young Terrance."

He nodded, knowing that he was inside a trap as firmly set as the pixie's.

"Then, maybe later, you could help me with my garden," she said, turning from him and looking around. "Egfrid was so wild, I thought…I thought that maybe if I gave him some structure, maybe he'd mellow. Then I kept it that way, to give my own grief a form to follow, instead of raging and destroying everything."

Terrance suddenly understood the tamed nature of her garden. It was a reminder to herself as well, to not let herself get too lost in her feelings.

"I'd like that," Terrance said. He took a look around. The bones of the garden were good. But he could easily seem a couple places where he could "wild it up some" as it were.

After saying goodbye, Terrance flew back into his own yard. Dad hoovered there in the center of it, waiting for him.

"She invited me over!" Terrance said before Dad could accuse him of anything. He flew closer, dropping his voice. "And she told me about her boys."

"Good," Dad said. "She's told so few fairies about what really happened."

"And she said that I can help her redo her garden!" Terrance said, remembering the best part of the conversation.

"That will be an excellent use of your talents," Dad said. "You really do have a knack for growing things," he added, looking with pride out on the garden they had.

"Thanks," Terrance said, feeling his ears wiggling with embarrassment.

Maybe he would become a master gardener someday. It sure beat trying to trap fairies into going astray. Though he had liked trying to solve the mystery…

He wasn't about to become a detective, not like those stupid shows produced by humans that didn't portray fairies accurately *at all.* Still, it was something to think about. Something more to do before he immersed himself in the trees and plants and soil that he loved.

And tomorrow, during the celebrations, he really would dance with Mrs. Smithers. See if he could get her to dance a little wildly, let go of her grief enough to feel the joy of living again.

It would be his own type of fairy trap that he could set.

MOSAIC MAGIC

AH, *nothing like the fresh smell of grout in the morning.*

Suzi giggled to herself as she dug her rubber float/trowel into the bucket, scooping out a hefty portion of the sandy paste.

It actually stank like cheap paint, with the dusty smell of concrete underneath. She still relished the scent, because it meant that she was nearly finished with this job. This was the last room in the new house that she had to tile, the huge living room.

She'd taken the job with a new-to-her general contractor. A pixie named Morning Blossom. Suzi had never worked for a non-Human general contractor before. For that matter, she'd never worked with pixies or other magical beings, either. She suspected this might be her last time.

The tiles she'd put in two days before looked like rich, red-tinted wood, almost a mahogany. They'd been oversized, nine inches by forty inches, like actual planks of wood, and had been a pain in the ass to do. Now, they were smoothly cemented to the subfloor, everything perfectly level, with evenly spaced grout lines between each "board."

Suzi had spent a little time that morning doing cleanup, removing mortar from the grout lines as well as wiping off the tiles, getting them damp. The grout she was applying was a dark brown color, called *coffee bean.*

Well, only if you liked your coffee well roasted. She preferred lighter roasts.

Suzi took her time with the first set of tiles, pushing the grout into the crevices between the tiles, then scraping off the excess. Next, she used a big, brand new grout sponge to clean off the remaining grout as well as to smooth out the grout lines.

She always liked this part, sweeping the sponge in circles over the tiles, getting all the lines just right. It was easy to get lost in this work.

Last step involved using a microfiber cloth. It was honestly the silliest thing she'd ever heard of, or had to do, as a tiler. However, it worked.

She dragged a semi-damp microfiber cloth across the face of the tiles, going at a forty-five degree angle, not following the grout lines. As this grout happened to be extra sandy, the microfiber cloth picked up what sand remained on the tile itself.

After the last swipe of the cloth, Suzi reassured herself that the trick had actually worked by running her hand across the surface of the smooth tile.

It wasn't actual magic. No, the fairies, brownies, and pixies (FBP) had the corner on that market. It just felt like magic, how dragging a cloth across the face of the tiles cleaned them right up.

Suzi reached behind her and picked up her handy shop light, shining it into the corner she was working on. New construction was sometimes harder than remodels. The building didn't have electricity in most of the rooms yet, and certainly no lights had been hung. So she had bring her own shop light everywhere to see her handiwork.

Everything looked good, the grout lines clean, the tile clear and not hazy. She dabbed a little more grout into the end of one of the cracks, next to the wall. It would be covered by the base molding, but she wanted to make sure.

Then she started on the next patch of floor. She found she could get all the way across the wide room once before she had to stop and clear her buckets, go outside and get fresh water.

That was always the limiting factor for grouting tile,

the access to fresh water. If she was working with someone, she'd have them refreshing her buckets after every section. As she was on her own that morning, it just meant regular breaks.

She was a little over halfway finished with the floor when she heard the angry buzzing noise that proclaimed that her pipsqueak boss, Morning Blossom, had arrived.

While Suzi had had micro-managing GCs before, Morning Blossom was particularly picky. Supposedly, Morning Blossom had been working as a GC for a while, building homes for Humans. And there were other Humans subcontractors for this project, who appeared to enjoy working for Morning Blossom, like the plumber and the electrician.

But there were also non-Humans who'd come in. Like the fairy who'd used magic to fill in the glass for the window frames. Not only were they naturally sparkling and clean, they let in more light during the day and kept out the cold at night. She'd heard that Morning Blossom had hired a large subcrew of brownies to do the framing. The electrician had talked about how one night, the foundation stood empty. Then, the next morning, half the walls had magically been raised up.

It felt to Suzi as if Morning Blossom was pickier about the tile work because she could see it. Plumbing and electricity were magic that happened behind the walls. It either worked (and passed inspection) or it didn't work. There wasn't anything the GC could do about it except call back the subcontractor.

Plus, if there ever was a mistake, Suzi couldn't just wave her hand and magically fix it. Like the fairies did who came in to paint the sheetrock the other day. They'd chosen the wrong color of mauve, at least according to Morning

Blossom. Instead of repainting, they'd just cast some magic to get the paint to change hues.

At least the FBP couldn't build Human houses without materials. Or help. It turned out that while they could magically raise a structure, the building wouldn't stay standing, not unless a constant trickle of magic was being fed to it. This meant that Human homes still required physical labor.

Which meant that Suzi always had a job working as a tiler. Particularly now, as it was summer in Seattle, the height of the building season.

Even if it did mean trying new GCs now and again.

And getting burned.

Morning Blossom came buzzing in. (And really, the FBP had been recognized by Humanity back after the All-Races riots in the 1970s. Why parents still insisted on traditional names for their kids, or the kids still used traditional names, was beyond Suzi.)

As a pixie, Morning Blossom possibly came up to Suzi's knee. She generally created an illusion of herself as larger when dealing with Humans. Today, she appeared to be a little over three feet tall. Her brown hair stuck out from the top of her head in all directions, as if she'd just crawled out from under a static-filled wool blanket. Her green eyes were overly large in her small, round face, and her ears stuck up on either side, like unfortunately mismatched handles.

From the strangely flat plane of her face, her nose rose abruptly, big and sharp. The teeth in her huge mouth were all pointed, like those of a cat.

Pixies didn't really eat Human children. They claimed that those were just old myths, used to keep the Humans at bay.

Suzi had to wonder sometimes, though, particularly after meeting Morning Blossom, and the way she smacked her lips together and looked at Suzi hungrily.

Other people described pixie fingers as twigs. It wasn't that they were so skinny and long, though they were. They also had multiple joints in each finger. Pixies could have as many as eight fingers to a hand, though Morning Blossom, in her illusionary form, only came with five.

Pixies, like the fairies, always appeared with wings. There had been concern of the members of the FBP impersonating Humans. However, there was some sort of psychological or physical barrier, and neither the pixies or the fairies would ever create an illusionary form that didn't have wings.

Fairy wings were doubled up, like a dragonfly's. Suzi had heard them described as equal parts gossamer and moonlight. Pixie wings were more like butterfly wings, looking more substantial, though they tended to be a single gray color, with ragged ends.

"What are you doing!!!!" Morning Blossom screeched as she flew into the living room.

Suzi sat back on her heels and looked at her GC. Morning Blossom was dressed in a T-shirt dress made out of a faded blue denim. Her wings took on the same hue that day. She looked like a particularly spoiled child, who Mommy and Daddy had pampered every day of her life.

"Grouting the floor," Suzi replied slowly. She didn't mean to sound patronizing. But if she didn't make herself talk slowly, taking pauses and deep breaths between her sentences, she'd end up screaming.

Morning Blossom always just bothered her *that much*.

"With that?" Morning Blossom said, wrinkling her nose at the smell.

All of the Little People, as the FBP were referred to collectively, had a much better sense of smell than a Human.

"Yes," Suzi said.

"It looks like mud," Morning Blossom said.

"It's the color the client requested," Suzi said. "I can pull up the work order to show you."

"But there's no…sparkle in it. No pizazz," the pixie complained.

Suzi shrugged. "It's what they wanted," she said again.

"Maybe just a hint of glitter?" Morning Blossom said, lifting her hand, threatening to engulf them all in a shower of sparkles.

"No," Suzi said firmly. "They want a nice, sedate floor for their living room."

"But they liked the sparkle that I added to the bedrooms upstairs," Morning Blossom pointed out.

"Those were for the children's rooms. Not the living room where they'll entertain other adults," Suzi said. She wasn't about to budge on this one. As a GC, Morning Blossom should know better than to do something other than what the client requested.

Fortunately (?) Morning Blossom dropped the idea as she came closer, inspecting Suzi's work.

"You missed a spot," Morning Blossom said, disapproval dripping down heavily. "The tile's still dirty from that awful grout."

"Where?" Suzi asked, though she knew she hadn't missed anything. "Don't touch it, just show me," she warned. While the tile itself had set, the grout was still wet. She didn't want anything disturbing her nice, clean lines.

"Right there," Morning Blossom said, hovering above a spot three feet back from where Suzi was currently working.

With a sigh, Suzi picked up her slightly damp microfiber cloth and slowly, carefully walked out across the tiles to the spot Morning Blossom indicated. She made sure to only step on the tiles themselves and to never get close to any of the grout lines. Fortunately, the big tiles made it easier than it normally would be.

There was, in fact, a small brown spot exactly where Morning Blossom was pointing. It made no sense, as it was perfectly round.

How could she have even made such a spot? Suzi balanced herself and folded over to wipe up the grout.

However, with the first pass of her cloth, she knew she'd been tricked.

She glared up at Morning Blossom, who just floated there, her wings slightly waving. "Made you look!" she declared gleefully.

Suzi growled at her, swallowing down the inappropriate curse words she wanted to let fly with.

"I need to finish this today," Suzi said as she carefully made her way back across the grouted floor to where her bucket and float awaited.

"But I have a proposition for you!" Morning Blossom proclaimed. "And if I hadn't gotten you to stop working, even for just a bit, you'd never hear me out."

Suzi made herself stop again. She folded her arms across her chest and stood, considering the pixie.

All right, she had to admit that she did get a little focused when she started working. Just a tiny bit lost in what she was doing. She didn't have a deadline—she just wanted to be finished with this job and take the rest of the afternoon off. Tomorrow, there was a different job site she'd travel to, to do the same thing.

"Have you heard of the building trades council new

project?" Morning Blossom asked. "They're looking for Human-FBP cooperative artwork."

Suzi nodded slowly. She had heard of it, actually. While the building trades council tended to be focused more on the practical side of things, this had sounded like an arty-farty project.

Suzi was a tiler. While she did create beautiful work, it wasn't art, not at least how most people defined it.

"So you'll be my partner?" Morning Blossom said. "I have the most amazing idea for a tiled mosaic—"

"What?" Suzi said. Surprise didn't even begin to cover her feeling.

"They're looking for works created by Human-FBP cooperation," Morning Blossom said. "Plus, it'll be a great way to get more business for both of us. Everyone will see the results if we place, even if we don't win. But we'd be a shoo-in."

"Why would you want to work with me?" Suzi asked, still befuddled. "I mean, you don't even like me."

She hadn't meant to say that out loud, but the words had just kind of come out.

"Of course I like you!" Morning Blossom said. Her wide mouth gaped in what could be called a grin. "Otherwise, I wouldn't tease you."

"Oh," Suzi said. Had that been what Morning Blossom called it? Questioning every decision that Suzi made in terms of her tilling work? Always pointing out flaws and non-existent issues?

"So you'll do it! Great," Morning Blossom said. She floated a piece of paper over toward Suzi's bucket. "Meet me here at seven PM and we can get started!"

Morning Blossom buzzed out of the room before Suzi could say another word.

Wait. What had just happened?

Had she just agreed to work on an art project with the GC from hell?

She sighed and walked over to where the piece of paper had landed, conveniently next to her float. The address wasn't too far from her loft apartment.

Great.

She knew better than to try and text Morning Blossom. She only answered her phone when it was a client, not someone on her crew.

Well, maybe Suzi should just ghost the pixie. Except that she didn't want that sort of reputation either, of not showing up for a gig. Word would get around.

Fine. She could show up at seven that evening. Explain that she was too busy, there were too many other things going on right now, she didn't have time. Something.

Anything but work with Morning Blossom again.

THE ADDRESS TURNED out to be a set of warehouses that had been turned into shared FBP art space. Though the neighborhood was slightly sketchy—on the wrong side of the major boulevard that separated the Capital Hill neighborhood from Central District in Seattle—it was still light out. Besides, while Humans might tolerate some level of crime in their neighborhoods, the FBP didn't.

It was remarkable how the FBP had changed the Human trajectory. Everyone, everywhere, had clean air and clean water. Any big project that might affect the environment had to get FBP approval. If a corporation tried going around them, the construction would run into so many problems it quickly became unsustainable.

Suzi had recently seen a documentary set in one of those places filled with "Human First" assholes, about how horrific those areas had become. They even had people who were homeless, sleeping in the streets! That just wasn't allowed anywhere else, anywhere civilized.

The nighttime belonged to the FBP, and Humans generally needed to be safely in their houses before sunset. As it was summer, sunset wouldn't be for another couple of hours, so Suzi had time.

It wasn't as hard of a rule in the city of Seattle, not like it was out in the suburbs. Plus, Suzi knew that in her neighborhood, she'd be fine as long as she stuck to the major streets.

The door to the warehouse was solid metal with a hint of a looping design etched into the bright silver. Would it show up better in sunlight? Or in moonlight? She suspected the latter. She heard the whine of a table saw and smelled fresh wood being cut in one of the workshops. She could also smell fresh paint.

When she pressed the doorbell for the workshop number Morning Blossom had given her, the door buzzed open right away.

What, had Morning Blossom been waiting for her? Possibly wondering if Suzi would show up?

Maybe Suzi could use that to her advantage.

The long hallway between the workshops was significantly cooler than the warm evening air outside. Suzi wasn't sure why, though she'd heard other people talk about the icy brilliance of magic. Was it enough to cool off an entire building?

Morning Blossom flung open the door as Suzi walked up to it. "You came! You came! You really came!" Morning Blossom squeaked.

She was pixie sized that evening, not much longer

than Suzi's arm. Everything else looked the same, though; the wild brown hair sticking out all over like a spiky mane; her overly-large green eyes which looked happier than Suzi could recall ever seeing; her butterfly-like wings the color of the new moon . Even her wide smile (and admittedly needle-sharp teeth) seemed almost warm and welcoming.

Morning Blossom wore a shift dress that was made from a thread-bare cotton, like a piece of clothing that had been washed and then left out to dry in the sunlight too many times. It was pale green with cute little yellow flowers on it, an old-fashioned pattern.

"Come here, come here and see!" Morning Blossom said, flying away from the door and into the studio.

Suzi paused for a moment, then shook her head and closed the door behind her before walking further into the large space.

The studio was longer than it was wider, with windows at the far end. Easels holding paintings lined the walls. They weren't realistic in the least, just splashes of color thrown on the canvas.

Except that they moved as Suzi walked by. She glanced quickly at one then steadfastly looked away. It wasn't that the artwork was dangerous or mesmerizing, but rather, disturbing, the way the colors flowed together and apart, just out of the corner of her eye, like mouths opening and shutting.

She told herself again that pixies didn't eat Humans, or if they did, they'd prefer Human children. Not tough older broads like her.

At the end of the workshop a large wooden frame lay on the concrete floor, maybe five foot on a side and a foot deep. A wooden subfloor material covered the front of it, looking out of place. Three heaps of stones were piled next to it. They were sorted by color, going from whitish to blackish, with grayish stones in between.

A bucket with Suzi's favorite pre-mixed mortar sat next to the piles. Two trowels—brand new versions of her scuffed up favorites—sat on the floor next to the bucket.

"What is this?" Suzi asked, taken back. How had Morning Blossom known what to get? Had she really been paying that much attention to Suzi?

"I figured we should practice together. At least once. To make sure that we can win," Morning Blossom said. She bobbed in the air as she was speaking, looking out the windows and not at Suzi.

The glass in the windows was a dull gray, reinforced with chicken wire. Though the windows took up most of the wall, rising from floor to ceiling, they really wouldn't let in much light.

They seemed impractical to Suzi, and she wasn't sure why Morning Blossom would have them in her studio. Maybe just the idea of windows was appealing?

"Practicing…what, exactly?" Suzi said, still trying to wrap her head around her micro-managing GC doing artwork. Painting in such a haphazard kind of way.

She glanced back at the canvases behind her, then quickly looked forward again. Yes, all those little mouths were focused on her, she was certain of it.

And there was so much red. Like blood.

Maybe this had been a mistake, walking into the lair of a pixie.

"For the contest," Morning Blossom said, sounding as patronizing as Suzi generally did.

"What exactly did you have in mind? For this art project?"

"I thought you could do a mosaic," Morning Blossom said, seeming to regain her enthusiasm.

Then again, that was one of the constant comments (complaints) about the FBP. They rarely stayed in a single emotional state for very long.

"A mosaic?" Suzi said, feeling stupid. "With these stones?" she guessed.

"Exactly!" Morning Blossom said, beaming at her.

"I don't do mosaics," Suzi said. "I do tile work."

"But it's like tile, right? Stones in mortar?" Morning Blossom said, obviously confused.

"Yes," Suzi said slowly. And all right, maybe she *had* done something like that before. High-end bathroom. Instead of a smooth basin for the floor of the shower, they'd wanted river stones embedded in a sea of mortar. Something about how stimulating it would be to take a shower and massage the soles of their feet.

Suzi hadn't created an artful pattern with those stones. Not really. She had tried to create a soothing yet stimulating piece instead. It must have worked, because she got three other jobs in the same neighborhood after that, remodeling bathrooms and kitchens.

Had Morning Blossom heard about that work? Possibly. The construction business wasn't really that big, and did operate a lot on word-of-mouth.

"What kind of pattern are you imagining?" Suzi asked reluctantly. This was far beyond the scope of the job they'd been doing.

Why had she agreed to this again?

No, wait, she hadn't. Not really.

"See, I was thinking a huge swirl," Morning Blossom said. "Coming in from the edges and forming a whirlpool in the center."

"How do we level it out?" Suzi said as she picked up a couple of the stones, weighing them in her hands. They weren't the same size, depth, height, width, what have you.

"Push it down further into the mortar," Morning Blossom said, as if the answer was obvious.

Suzi sighed. "This isn't going to work," she said.

"You haven't even tried it yet!" Morning Blossom complained.

"Why me?" Suzi said, putting down the stones and turning to look at Morning Blossom. "I mean, I went and read the specs for the contest this afternoon. We are supposed to be able to work together. This was the first job I'd ever worked with you on."

"Yes, but, you didn't run away screaming after my comments on the bathroom," Morning Blossom said, preening. "You even seemed to incorporate some of them in the kitchen."

Suzi opened her mouth for a harsh retort, then closed it again. "I signed a contract," Suzi pointed out. "I don't walk out on those." She never had. She'd always fulfilled the work she'd signed up for.

Even when she ended up in the hole for a job and it hadn't been her fault.

"So let's sign a contract and get to work!" Morning Blossom said, going back to being overly enthusiastic.

"What exactly is your part in all this?" Suzi said. She wasn't about to sign another contract with the pixie. She was, however, curious about what exactly the pixie was proposing.

"Don't you worry about that," Morning Blossom said dismissively.

"No, if this is a collaboration, then I do get to worry about it," Suzi replied. She crossed her arms over her chest and leaned back slightly on her heels.

Working in the construction business, generally with a bunch of pig-headed men, had taught her how to be more stubborn than most people. Her last boyfriend had accused her of being the most stubborn woman he'd ever met.

If she could only find someone who's say that and mean it as a positive thing…

"All right. Fine. It's magic, okay?" Morning Blossom said. "I'll animate the whirlpool. Make it come alive."

Suzi couldn't help gulping slightly, though she did have enough control to not look over her shoulder at the paintings behind her.

"Won't that be disturbing?" she asked.

"No, no, it'll be fine. It'll just draw people in, you know? Hold them there," Morning Blossom assured her.

"I'm still not sure that sounds like a good idea," Suzi said. "These are trades people who you're working with. Not art critics."

"Then why would they sponsor an art show?" Morning Blossom asked reasonably.

Suzi had wondered the same thing, and had spent some time reading between the lines. "They're looking more for art installations, as it were. Pieces that high-paying clients would buy as part of the architectural package. This…I suppose, maybe, you could hang it on a wall…"

"So let's do it!" Morning Blossom said. "I tried to get everything right. The mortar. The trowels. Right?"

"You did good," Suzi said. Was her control-freak of a GC actually just looking for a little praise?

Morning Blossom beamed at Suzi. "Yay!" She did a backflip in the air, her wings vibrating madly.

Suzi opened up the bucket of mortar. It was a gray color, which would offset both the white and the black rocks, as well as most of the shades of gray ones.

The smell did perk her up slightly.

Here goes nothing. Suzi kept the words to herself. Maybe it would all work out in the end.

And maybe pigs would sprout wings like the FBP.

"NO, NOT THAT ONE, THIS ONE," Morning Blossom said, thrusting a stone toward Suzi.

Exasperated, Suzi sat back on her heels, trowel in one hand, stone in the other. She looked at Morning Blossom, then back at the "artwork" they'd been trying to do.

The design wasn't very creative, or at least Suzi didn't think so. Though some might call what she did artistic, she didn't ever consider it art.

They had started the piece with a band of gray stones flaring out where it met the frame of the piece, then narrowing as it curved toward the center. Suzi had added a small band of black stones, then begun doing the same sort of band with the white.

But Morning Blossom kept interrupting her, telling her to use different stones than the ones she had at hand.

"Why?" Suzi demanded angrily. "What is the difference between this stone and that one?"

Morning Blossom looked guilty. "I don't know. I just like this one better."

"No," Suzi said. "That isn't good enough. Either explain your logic to me or stop trying to dictate what I'm doing."

Morning Blossom looked a little lost and hurt.

"Do I tell you how to do your magic?" Suzi asked.

"No?" Morning Blossom said, sounding hesitant.

"You are correct. I do not. Because I don't know a thing about it," Suzi said. "Now, look at the stone in my hand. See the curve on this side?"

The stone she held was white and flat. One side was almost straight, while the top part of it curved. It felt cool against her skin, and only had a little bit of roughness across the bottom of it.

"This will fit perfectly here," Suzi said, defiantly placing the stone into the mortar. "Its shape matches the curve that I have going on here. Do you see it?"

Morning Blossom nodded slowly, then shook her head. "No. This stone would have been just as good."

Suzi took the stone from Morning Blossom. "No, it wouldn't have," Suzi said. "It wouldn't have worked with the curve I have going here."

"Maybe the curve is wrong," Morning Blossom said stubbornly.

"You know what? I give up," Suzi said, standing. "I've tried to be accommodating. This is supposed to be a collaboration. That means we both contribute to it."

"That's what I was trying to do!" Morning Blossom complained. "I was trying to contribute!"

"But I thought your contribution was going to be the magic, afterward," Suzi pointed out.

"Oh. Yeah. There's that," Morning Blossom said. She sighed and looked defeated, her wings drooping, her toes pointing toward the ground. Even her hair deflated, flopping down over her eyes.

"You're not very good at collaborating, are you?" Suzi said, her tone more gentle.

Morning Blossom looked up, her green eyes lit with anger. "Who says?"

"I say," Suzi said. She tried to add a laugh, but it sounded more like an angry bark. "However, I'll let you in on a secret. I'm not good at it either."

"I thought everyone in the construction business was good at it!" Morning Blossom said, looking puzzled.

"That's what the building trades council said in their brochure."

Suzi snorted. "They lied," she said blandly. "There are just as many 'I can do it on my own' workers as there are people who genuinely work well with others."

As well as pig-headed assholes, but Suzi didn't actually think Morning Blossom was of that ilk. Just...micro-managing and clueless.

Morning Blossom looked at the work that Suzi had already done, to the pile of stones, then to Suzi.

"So what do we do now?" she asked plaintively. "I'd still like to enter the contest. Better yet, I'd like to win."

"Why?" Suzi said, sensing that there was a story here. "Why does it matter to you?"

Morning Blossom looked down again, almost shy. "You know how hard it is, as a woman in the trades. It's even harder as an FBP. Working with your hands, unless it's a traditional task, is *not* looked upon well."

"What do pixies generally create?" Suzi said. She knew that the brownies were famous for their shoes and other fashion accessories. Fairies were good for potions and any kind of cooking.

"Toys," Morning Blossom said softly. "I know that supposedly Santa has elves, but what he really has are pixies."

"I didn't know that," Suzi said. She was sure it was documented somewhere, but honestly, no one really went in for handmade toys anymore. Particularly not if they weren't the offshoot of some mega-movie or cartoon.

"Wait. Does that mean Santa's real?" Suzi had to ask suddenly. Elves, trolls, vampires, and most of the other creatures man had written about over the years had turned out to be just myths, thankfully, though the consensus about ghosts was far from unanimous.

"I don't want to just build toys," Morning Blossom said, ignoring Suzi's question. "I wanted to build houses. Real things."

"This contest isn't about building real things, but art. And cooperation," Suzi pointed out.

"I know." Morning Blossom sighed, looking down and away again, as if unable to meet Suzi's eye. "I'd be able to show the award to my parents. They wouldn't understand, but maybe they'd be proud of me."

Suzi's bit back her first response because it wasn't polite and it involved a lot of profanity about how a child shouldn't have to "prove" anything to their parents. Then again, her parents had always encouraged her to do whatever she wanted. Her father had given her great advice about dealing with the chauvinistic men, making them explain their "jokes" to her. She didn't have to be twice as good as any of the guys in order to be successful, but she'd still had to put up with her share of crap.

"All right," Suzi finally responded slowly. "But I'm still not sure how to make this work. It doesn't feel like we're cooperating at all, you know? More like I'm doing something, than you're changing it. We aren't…flowing."

Morning Blossom shrugged. "I don't know how to work anyway else. As you said, you don't know anything about magic."

"True. But I can direct you, just as you can direct me, right?" Suzi said.

"I guess…" Morning Blossom said, looking to the side again.

"Do you really want to win this?" Suzi said, standing up and going over to where Morning Blossom hovered, closer to the windows.

"More than anything," Morning Blossom said solemnly, her eyes wide.

Suzi doubted it. She knew that the FPB were mercurial, that while Morning Blossom might prioritize this contest currently, there was a good chance she'd forget about it in a week.

Then again, she had already done a lot of work, gathering supplies, paying attention to Suzi and getting the right tools.

"Then let's try to work on this together," Suzi suggested. "Tell me more about the magic. And I'll tell you more about the tiling process. Maybe we can figure it out."

"All right…" Morning Blossom said. She floated a rock up and pushed it toward Suzi. "Feel that."

Suzi nearly gasped at the shock of cold that went through her fingers, then quickly dissipated. "Why is magic cold?" she said.

Morning Blossom shrugged. "Saw some crazy theory once that we're dipping into a different dimension in order to move things. So that's the cold of space."

"Cool," Suzi said.

Morning Blossom just rolled her eyes at the pun.

Suzi went back to the frame. "Could you float a few more over this way?" she said as she kneeled back down.

Morning Blossom sent a few over, and had them rotate slowly around Suzi. She was able to snag one from the air and put it into the perfect spot, then the next one.

"Hey, this is actually going to go much faster this way," she commented after she place a few more.

"Then let's pick up the pace," Morning Blossom said with a wicked grin.

It was Suzi's turn to roll her eyes.

While she and Morning Blossom were never going to see eye to eye on most things, they could still work together on this.

And maybe get a prize to boot.

SUZI COULDN'T TAKE her eyes away from the huge screen that stood next to their finished art piece. They were at the event center near the baseball stadium, at the Home Show. The tall, echoing ceiling buzzed with wings of the Little People flying overhead, while louder Human conversation carried on below.

The air smelled of industrial grease, freshly cut wood, and a few chemical components, like the cleaner that she'd seen advertised at the end of the row that she'd rather chew nails than use.

The Builder's Competition took up one huge end of the room. While theirs certainly wasn't the most extravagant, the video next to the piece certainly was.

It showed Suzi sitting on the side of the art piece, dozens of stones circling her slowly. All she had to do was pluck one out of the air then set it into the mortar she'd already spread.

In the video, Suzi appeared to be meditating. She didn't remember this part of it, just that she'd been in the zone. It showed. Every movement was deliberate. Nothing was wasted. Every stone fit perfectly. There was no second guessing.

The video, more than the art piece, showed true cooperation between a pixie and a Human.

The piece was pretty enough, with the bands of black, white, and gray elegantly curving in toward the center. It was a statement piece, but not very colorful. It had won second place, the blue ribbon on the side of it proudly proclaiming the fact.

First place had gone to the glass waterfall arrangement. It was made up of several glass rods that all glowed with a opalescent hue. Water traveled up inside the rods, then splashed down, either into beautiful shells or onto other rods. The sound of the water dripping was perfectly enchanting.

The video showing the making of that installation also showed cooperation, Suzi had to admit, with the Human and the Fairy consulting and making plans. Some of the rods were blown by the Human, others by the Fairy. It was a charming video showing two friends working side by side.

Suzi wondered if that was all a pretense, though, as she'd yet to see the two be friendly to each other in the hall.

"There you are!" Morning Blossom said, flitting down to hover next to Suzi. "It's great, isn't it?"

"It actually is really nice," Suzi said. "Thank you for asking me to create this with you."

"So many business cards flying off the shelf!" Morning Blossom exclaimed.

Suzi nodded. That had been the real reason behind this venture, was to get both of them more business.

From the way her phone had already started ringing, Suzi knew that she would have her pick in terms of jobs.

"I'm sorry that we didn't win first prize," Suzi said. "I know that would have meant a lot to you." Because while the work coming in was good, the recognition was what Morning Blossom had been all about.

Morning Blossom shook her head. "My parents came to the show, and saw my work," she said softly. "They liked it."

From the expression of wonder that filled Morning Blossom's face, Suzi knew that was the real prize.

"I'm glad," Suzi said.

"And, more importantly, the piece has sold!" Morning Blossom said. "There's a new subdivision going up. High end. They're looking for someone to do all the tile and stone work..."

Suzi nodded slowly. It would mean constant work for a few months. But did she really want to commit to a single gig that way? Then she shook her head. No, she'd be happier sticking with smaller, personal jobs.

"Good," Morning Blossom said. "I didn't want to take it either. But what are we going to do next?"

"We?" Suzi asked, surprised. While they'd eventually worked well together, it wasn't the sort of thing that they could do all the time.

"I've proposed that we do mosaics for the walkways and parks of the new subdivision. Better pay. And we'd work together!"

Suzi opened her mouth, then shut it again. "You'd want to work with me?" she said slowly.

Morning Blossom gave her an earnest nod. "Yes. You didn't walk out on me. You helped me figure out how to work with someone, instead of just ordering them around or doing it myself. We're pieces that fit together."

Suzi had to smile at the image. While it had taken some time, they had eventually gotten into the flow of things.

"Besides, if we spend more time working together, then next year, we'll be able to blow away all the competition!" Morning Blossom said, twirling.

Suzi rolled her eyes at that. The council wasn't likely to offer the exact same challenge every year.

Still, she supposed that she was up for the challenge.

"Let me know the reply to your proposal," Suzi said after a few moments.

"All right. Partner," Morning Blossom said, her entire body glowing as if suffused with sunlight.

After saying goodbye, Suzi headed out of the hallway,

back toward the exit. This wasn't what she'd expected from taking her first FBP job. But it fit, somehow, with the rest of her life.

Disparate materials, matched together.

Mosaic magic.

ABOUT THE AUTHOR

Leah Cutter tells page-turning, wildly creative stories that always leave you guessing in the middle, but completely satisfied by the end.

She writes mystery of all sorts. Her Lake Hope cozy mysteries have been well received by readers, who just want to curl up and have tea with the main character. Her Halley Brown series, revolving around a private investigator who used to be with the Seattle Police Department, leave you guessing at every turn. And her speculative mysteries, such as the Alvin Goodfellow Case Files—a 1930s PI set on the moon—have garnered great reviews.

She's been published in magazines such as *Alfred Hitchcock's Mystery Magazine* and in anthologies like *Fiction River: Spies.* On top of that, Leah is the editor of the new quarterly mystery magazine: *Mystery, Crime, and Mayhem.*

Find Leah's books on Knotted Road Press at www.KnottedRoadPress.com

Follow her blog at www.LeahCutter.com.

Read more mysteries at www.MysteryCrimeAndMayhem.com.

Reviews

It's true. Reviews help me sell more books. If you've

enjoyed this story, please consider leaving a review of it on your favorite site.

Come someplace new…

Are you a traveler? Do you enjoy exploring strange new worlds, new cultures, new people?

Journey into the various lands envisioned by Leah Cutter.

Sign up for my newsletter and I'll start you on your travels with a free copy of my book, *The Island Sampler.*

I will never spam you or use your email for nefarious purposes. You can also unsubscribe at any time.

http://www.LeahCutter.com/newsletter/

ABOUT KNOTTED ROAD PRESS

Knotted Road Press fiction specializes in dynamic writing set in mysterious, exotic locations.

Knotted Road Press non-fiction publishes autobiographies, business books, cookbooks, and how-to books with unique voices.

Knotted Road Press creates DRM-free ebooks as well as high-quality print books for readers around the world.

With authors in a variety of genres including literary, poetry, mystery, fantasy, and science fiction, Knotted Road Press has something for everyone.

Knotted Road Press
www.KnottedRoadPress.com

www.ingramcontent.com/pod-product-compliance
Lightning Source LLC
Chambersburg PA
CBHW070042130726
47907CB00017B/1344

* 9 7 8 1 6 4 4 7 0 2 8 1 9 *